THE LION OF THE NORTH

A TALE OF THE TIMES OF
GUSTAVUS ADOLPHUS AND THE WARS OF RELIGION

VOLUME ONE

by
G.A. HENTY

Author of
The Boy Knight
In Freedom's Cause

and others

Illustrated by John Shonberg

Schmul Publishing Co.
Schmul's Wesleyan Book Club ● Salem, Ohio ● 1996

Copyright © 1996 by Schmul Publishing Co.
All rights reserved.

Published by Schmul Publishing Co.
PO Box 716
Salem, Ohio 44460

Printed by Old Paths Tract Society
RR2, Box 43
Shoals, Indiana 47581

ISBN 0-88019-355-7

PREFACE.

My Dear Lads: You are nowadays called upon to acquire so great a mass of learning and information in the period of life between the ages of twelve and eighteen that it is not surprising that but little time can be spared for the study of the history of foreign nations. Most lads are, therefore, lamentably ignorant of the leading events of even the most important epochs of Continental history, although, as many of these events have exercised a marked influence upon the existing state of affairs in Europe, a knowledge of them is far more useful, and, it may be said, far more interesting than that of the comparatively petty affairs of Athens, Sparta, Corinth, and Thebes.

Prominent among such epochs is the Thirty Years' War, which arose from the determination of the Emperor of Austria to crush out Protestantism throughout Germany. Since the invasion of the Huns no struggle which has taken place in Europe has approached this in the obstinacy of the fighting and the terrible sufferings which the war inflicted upon the people at large. During these thirty years the population of Germany decreased by nearly a third, and in some of the states half the towns and two-thirds of the villages absolutely disappeared.

The story of the Thirty Years' War is too long to be treated in one volume. Fortunately it divides itself naturally into two parts. The first begins with the entry of Sweden, under her chivalrous monarch Gustavus Adolphus, upon the struggle, and terminates with his death and that of his great rival Wallenstein. This portion of the war has been treated in the present story. The second period begins at the point when France assumed the leading part in the struggle, and concludes with the peace which secured liberty of conscience to the Protestants of Germany. This period I hope to treat some day in another story, so that you may have a complete picture of the war. The military events of the present tale, the battles, sieges, and operations, are all taken from the best authorities, while for the account of the special doings of Mackay's, afterward Munro's Scottish Regiment, I am indebted to Mr. J. Grant's "Life of Sir John Hepburn."

Yours sincerely,
G. A. HENTY.

CONTENTS.

CHAPTER I.
PAGE.
The Invitation.. 7

CHAPTER II.
Shipwrecked.. 25

CHAPTER III.
Sir John Hepburn.. 42

CHAPTER IV.
New Brandenburg.. 61

CHAPTER V.
Marauders... 79

CHAPTER VI.
The Attack on the Village................................... 95

CHAPTER VII.
A Quiet Time.. 113

CHAPTER VIII.
The Siege of Mansfeld....................................... 130

CHAPTER IX.
The Battle of Breitenfeld................................... 148

CONTENTS.

CHAPTER X.
PAGE.
The Passage of the Rhine........................... 166

CHAPTER XI.
The Capture of Oppenheim......................... 184

CHAPTER XII.
The Passage of the Lech............................ 202

CHAPTER XIII.
Captured by the Peasants........................... 219

CHAPTER XIV.
In the Church Tower................................ 237

CHAPTER XV.
A Timely Rescue.................................... 254

CHAPTER XVI.
The Siege of Nuremberg............................ 273

CHAPTER XVII.
The Death of Gustavus.............................. 291

CHAPTER XVIII.
Wounded.. 308

CHAPTER XIX.
A Pause in Hostilities............................... 321

CHAPTER XX.
Friends in Trouble.................................. 333

CHAPTER XXI.
Flight... 351

CONTENTS.

CHAPTER XXII.
PAGE.
The Conspiracy.. 371

CHAPTER XXIII.
The Murder of Wallenstein...... 387

CHAPTER XXIV.
Malcolm's Escape.... 405

CHAPTER XXV.
Nordlingen... 422

Malcolm and Grant cross the Rhine at midnight.—Page 184.
—*The Lion of the North*.

THE LION OF THE NORTH.

CHAPTER I.

THE INVITATION.

It was late in the afternoon in the spring of the year 1630; the hilltops of the south of Scotland were covered with masses of cloud, and a fierce wind swept the driving rain before it with such force that it was not easy to make way against it. It had been raining for three days without intermission. Every little mountain burn had become a boiling torrent, while the rivers had risen above their banks and flooded the low lands in the valleys.

The shades of evening were closing in, when a lad of some sixteen years of age stood gazing across the swollen waters of the Nith rushing past in turbid flood. He scarce seemed conscious of the pouring rain; but with his lowland bonnet pressed down over his eyes, and his plaid wrapped tightly round him, he stood on a rising hummock of ground at the edge of the flood, and looked across the stream.

"If they are not here soon," he said to himself, "they will not get across the Nith to-night. None but bold riders could do so now; but by what uncle says, Captain Hume must be that and more. Ah! here they come."

As he spoke two horsemen rode down the opposite side of the valley and halted at the water's edge. The prospect was not a pleasant one. The river was sixty or seventy feet wide, and in the center the water swept along in a raging current.

"You cannot cross here," the boy shouted at the top of his voice. "You must go higher up where the water's deeper."

The wind swept his words away, but his gestures were understood.

"The boy is telling us to go higher up," said one of the horsemen.

"I suppose he is," the other replied; "but here is the ford. You see the road we have traveled ends here, and I can see it again on the other side. It is getting dark, and were we to cross higher up we might lose our way and get bogged; it is years since I was here. What's the boy going to do now? Show us a place for crossing?"

The lad, on seeing the hesitation of the horsemen, had run along the bank up the stream, and to their surprise, when he had gone a little more than a hundred yards, he dashed into the water. For a time the water was shallow, and he waded out until he reached the edge of the regular bank of the river, and then swam out into the current.

"Go back," the horseman shouted; but his voice did not reach the swimmer, who, in a few strokes, was in the full force of the stream, and was soon lost to the sight of the horsemen among the short foaming waves of the torrent.

"The boy will be drowned," one of the horsemen said, spurring his horse up the valley; but in another minute the lad was seen breasting the calmer water just above the ford.

"You cannot cross here, Captain Hume," he said, as he approached the horsemen. "You must go nigh a mile up the river."

"Why, who are you, lad?" the horseman asked, "and how do you know my name?"

"I'm the nephew of Nigel Græme. Seeing how deep the floods were I came out to show you the way, for the best horse in the world could not swim the Nith here now."

"But this is the ford," Captain Hume said.

"Yes, this is the ford in dry weather. The bottom here is hard rock and easy to ride over when the river is but waist-deep, but below and above this place it is covered with great boulders. The water is six feet deep here now, and the horses would be carried down among the rocks, and would never get across. A mile up the river is always deep, and though the current is strong there is nothing to prevent a bold horseman from swimming across."

"I thank you heartily, young sir," Captain Hume said. "I can see how broken is the surface of the water, and doubt not that it would have fared hard with us had we attempted to swim across here. In faith, Munro, we have had a narrow escape."

"Ay, indeed," the other agreed. "It would have been hard if you and I, after going through all the battlefields of the Low Countries, should have been drowned here together in a Scottish burn. Your young friend is a gallant lad and a good swimmer, for in truth it was no light task to swim that torrent with the water almost as cold as ice."

"Now, sirs, will you please to ride on," the boy said; "it is getting dark fast, and the sooner we are across the better."

So saying he went off at a fast run, the horses trotting behind him. A mile above he reached the spot he had spoken of. The river was narrower here, and the stream was running with great rapidity, swirling and heaving as it went, but with a smooth, even surface.

"Two hundred yards farther up," the boy said, "is the beginning of the deep; if you take the water there you will get across so as to climb up by that sloping bank just opposite."

He led the way to the spot he indicated, and then plunged into the stream, swimming quietly and steadily across, and allowing the stream to drift him down. The horseman followed his example. They had swum many a swollen river, and although their horses snorted and plunged at first, they soon quieted down and swam steadily over. They just struck the spot which the boy had indicated. He had already arrived there, and, without a word, trotted forward.

It was soon dark, and the horsemen were obliged

to keep close to his heels to see his figure. It was as much as they could do to keep up with him, for the ground was rough and broken, sometimes swampy sometimes strewn with boulders.

"It is well we have a guide," Colonel Munro said to his companion; "for assuredly, even had we got safely across the stream, we should never have found our way across such a country as this. Scotland is a fine country, Hume, a grand country, and we are all proud of it, you know, but for campaigning, give me the plains of Germany; while, as for your weather here, it is only fit for a water-rat."

Hume laughed at this outburst.

"I shan't be sorry, Munro, for a change of dry clothes and a corner by a fire; but we must be nearly there now if I remember right. Græme's hold is about three miles from the Nith."

The boy presently gave a loud shout, and a minute later lights were seen ahead, and in two or three minutes the horsemen drew up at a door beside which two men were standing with torches; another strolled out as they stopped.

"Welcome, Hume! I am glad indeed to see you; and—ah! is it you, Munro? it is long indeed since we met."

"That it is, Græme; it is twelve years since we were students together at St. Andrew's."

"I did not think you would have come on such a night," Græme said.

"I doubt that we should have come to-night, or

any other night, Nigel, if it had not been that that brave boy who calls you uncle swam across the Nith to show us the best way to cross. It was a gallant deed, and I consider we owe him our lives."

"It would have gone hard with you, indeed, had you tried to swim the Nith at the ford; had I not made so sure you would not come I would have sent a man down there. I missed Malcolm after dinner, and wondered what had become of him. But come in and get your wet things off. It is a cold welcome keeping you here. My men will take your horses round to the stable and see that they are well rubbed down and warmly littered."

In a quarter of an hour the party were assembled again in the sitting-room. It was a bare room with heavily timbered ceiling and narrow windows high up from the ground, for the house was built for purposes of defense, lime most Scottish residences in those days. The floor was thickly strewn with rushes. Arms and trophies of the chase hung on the walls, and a bright fire blazing on the hearth gave it a warm and cheerful aspect. As his guests entered the room Græme presented them with a large silver cup of hot tea.

"Drain this," he said, "to begin with. I will warrant me a draught of hot tea will drive the cold of the Nith out of your bones."

The travelers drank off the cups.

"'Tis a famous drink," Hume said, "and there is nowhere I enjoy it so much as in Scotland, for the cold here seems to have a knack of getting into one's very marrow, though I will say there have been times in the Low Countries when we have appreciated such a draught. Well, and how goes it with you, Græme?"

"Things might be better; in fact, times in Scotland have been getting worse and worse ever since King James went to England, and all the court with him. If it were not for an occasional raid among the wild folks of Galloway, and a few quarrels among ourselves, life would be too dull to bear here."

"But why bear it?" Captain Hume asked. "You used to have plenty of spirit in our old college days, Græme, and I wonder at your rusting your life out here when there is a fair field and plenty of honor, to say nothing of hard cash, to be won in the Low Country. Why, beside Hepburn's regiment, which has made a itself a name throughout all Europe, there are half a score of Scottish regiments in the service of the king of Sweden, and his gracious majesty, Gustavus Adolphus, does not keep them idle, I warrant you."

"I have thought of going a dozen times," Græme said, "but you see circumstances have kept me back; but I have all along intended to cross the seas when Malcolm came of an age to take the charge of his father's lands. When my brother James was dying from that swordthrust he got in a fray with the Duffs, I promised him I would be a father to the boy, and see that he got his rights."

"Well, we will talk of the affair after supper, Græme, for now that I have got rid of the cold I begin to perceive that I am well-nigh famished."

As the officer was speaking, the servitors were laying the table, and supper was soon brought in. After ample justice had been done to this, and the board was again cleared, the three men drew their seats round the fire, Malcolm seating himself on a low stool by his uncle.

"And now to business, Nigel," Colonel Munro said. "We have not come back to Scotland to see the country, or to enjoy your weather, or even for the pleasure of swimming your rivers in flood. We are commissioned by the king of Sweden to raise some three thousand or four thousand more Scottish troops. I believe that the king intends to take part in the war in Germany, where the Protestants are getting terribly mauled, and where, indeed, it is likely that the Reformed religion will be stamped out altogether unless the Swedes strike in to their rescue. My chief object is to fill up to its full strength of two thousand men the Mackay Regiment of which I am lieutenant-colonel. The rest of the recruits whom we may get will go as drafts to fill up the vacancies in the other regiments. So you see here we are, and it is our intention to beat up all our friends and relations, and ask them each to raise a company or half a company of recruits, of which, of course, they would have the command.

"We landed at Berwick, and wrote to several of our friends that we were coming. Scott of Jedburgh

Colonel Munro seeks to enlist Nigel Græme and his nephew.—Page 15.
—*The Lion of the North.*

has engaged to raise a company. Balfour of Lauderdale, who is a cousin of mine, has promised to bring another; they were both at St. Andrew's with us, as you may remember, Græme. Young Hamilton, who has been an ensign in my regiment, left us on the way. He will raise a company in Douglasdale. Now, Græme, don't you think you can bring us a band of the men of Nithsdale?"

"I don't know," Græme said hesitatingly. "I should like it of all things, for I am sick of doing nothing here, and my blood often runs hot when I read of the persecutions of the Protestants in Germany; but I don't think I can manage it."

"Oh, nonsense, Nigel!" said Hume; "you can manage it easily enough if you have the will. Are you thinking of the lad there? Why not bring him with you? He is young, certainly, but he could carry a color; and as for his spirit and bravery, Munro and I will vouch for it."

"Oh, do, uncle," the lad exclaimed, leaping to his feet in his excitement. "I promise you I would not give you any trouble; and as for marching, there isn't a man in Nithsdale who can tire me out across the mountains."

"But what's to become of the house, Malcolm, and the land and the herds?"

"Oh, they will be all right," the boy said. "Leave old Duncan in charge, and he will look after them."

"But I had intended you to go to St. Andrew's next year, Malcolm, and I think the best plan will be for you to go there at once. As you say, Duncan can look after the place."

Malcolm's face fell.

"Take the lad with you, Græme," Colonel Munro said. "Three years under Gustavus will do him vastly more good than will St. Andrew's. You know it never did us any good to speak of. We learned a little more Latin than we knew when we went there, but I don't know that that has been of any use to us; whereas for the dry tomes of divinity we waded through, I am happy to say that not a single word of the musty stuff remains in my brains. The boy will see life and service, he will have opportunities of distinguishing himself under the eye of the most chivalrous king in Europe, he will have entered a noble profession, and have a fair chance of bettering his fortune, all of which is a thousand times better than settling down here in this corner of Scotland."

"I must think it over," Græme said; "it is a serious step to take. I had thought of his going to the court at London after he left the university, and of using our family interest to push his way there."

"What is he to do in London?" Munro said. "The old pedant James, who wouldn't spend a shilling or raise a dozen men to aid the cause of his own daughter, and who thought more of musty dogmatic treatises than of the glory and credit of the country he ruled over, or the sufferings of his co-religionists in Germany, has left no career open to a lad of spirit."

"Well, I will think it over by the morning," Græme said. "And now tell me a little more about the merits of this quarrel in Germany. If I am going to fight, I should like at least to know exactly what I am fighting about."

"My dear fellow," Hume laughed, "you will never make a soldier if you always want to know the ins and outs of every quarrel you have to fight about; but for once the tenderest conscience may be satisfied as to the justice of the contention. But Munro is much better versed in the history of the affair than I am; for, to tell you the truth, beyond the fact that it is a general row between the Protestants and Catholics, I have not troubled myself much in the matter."

"You must know," Colonel Munro began, "that some twenty years ago the Protestant princes of Germany formed a league for mutual protection and support, which they called the Protestant Union; and a year later the Catholics, on their side, constituted what they called the Holy League. At that time the condition of the Protestants was not unbearable. In Bohemia, where they constituted two-thirds of the population, Rudolph II., and after him Mathias, gave conditions of religious freedom.

"Gradually, however, the Catholic party about the emperor gained the upper hand, then various acts in breach of the conditions granted to the Protestants were committed, and public spirit on both sides became much embittered. On the 23d of May, 1618, the Estates of Bohemia met at Prague, and the Protestant nobles, headed by Count Thurn, came there armed, and demanded from the Imperial councilors an account of the high-handed proceedings. A violent quarrel ensued, and finally the Protestant deputies seized the councilors Martinitz and Slavata, and their secretary, and hurled them from the window into the dry ditch, fifty feet below. Fortunately for the councilors the ditch contained a quantity of light rubbish, and they and their secretary escaped without serious damage. The incident, however, was the commencement of war. Bohemia was almost independent of Austria, administering its own internal affairs. The Estates invested Count Thurn with the command of the army. The Protestant Union supported Bohemia in its action. Mathias, who was himself a tolerant and well-meaning man, tried to allay the storm; but, failing to do so, marched an army into Bohemia.

"Had Mathias lived matters would probaby have arranged themselves, but he died the following spring, and was succeeded by Ferdinand II. Ferdinand is one of the most bigoted Catholics living, and is at the same time a bold and resolute man; and he had taken a solemn vow at the shrine of Loretto that, if ever he came to the throne, he would re-establish Catholicism throughout his dominions. Both parties prepared for the strife; the Bohemians renounced their allegiance to him and nominated the Elector Palatine Frederick V., the husband of our Scotch princess, their king.

"The first blow was struck at Zablati. There a Union army, led by Mansfeldt, was defeated by the Imperial general Bucquoi. A few days later, however, Count Thurn, marching through Moravia and Upper Austria, laid siege to Vienna. Ferdinand's own subjects were estranged from him, and the cry of the Protestant army, 'Equal rights for all Christian churches,' was approved by the whole population—for even in Austria itself there were a very large number of Protestants. Ferdinand had but a few soldiers, the population of the city were hostile, and had Thurn only entered the town he could have seized the emperor without any resistance.

"Thurn hesitated, and endeavored instead to obtain the conditions of toleration which the Protestants required; and sixteen Austrian barons in the city were in the act of insisting upon Ferdinand signing these when the head of the relieving army entered the city. Thurn retired hastily. The Catholic princes and representatives met at Frankfort and elected Ferdinand Emperor of Germany. He at once entered into a strict agreement with Maximilian of Bavaria to crush Protestantism throughout Germany. The Bohemians, however, in concert with Bethlem Gabor, king of Hungary, again besieged Vienna; but as the winter set in they were obliged to retire. From that moment the Protestant cause was lost; Saxony and Hesse-Darmstadt left the Union aud joined Ferdinand. Denmark, which had promised its assistance to the

Protestants, was persuaded to remain quiet. Sweden was engaged in a war with the Poles.

"The Protestant army was assembled at Ulm; the army of the League, under the order of Maximilian of Bavaria, was at Donauwörth. Maximilian worked upon the fears of the Protestant princes, who, frightened at the contest they had undertaken, agreed to a peace, by which they bound themselves to afford no aid to Frederick V.

"The Imperial forces then marched to Bohemia and attacked Frederick's army outside Prague, and in less than an hour completely defeated it. Frederick escaped with his family to Holland. Ferdinand then took steps to carry out his oath. The religious freedom granted by Mathias was abolished. In Bohemia, Moravia, Silesia, and Austria proper many of the promoters of the rebellion were punished in life and property. The year following all members of the Calvinistic sect were forced to leave their country, a few months afterward the Lutherans were also expelled, and in 1627 the exercise of all religious forms except those of the Catholic Church was forbidden; two hundred of the noble, and thirty thousand of the wealthier and industrial classes, were driven into exile; and lands and property to the amount of £5,000,000 or £6,000,000 were confiscated.

"The hereditary dominions of Frederick V. were invaded, the Protestants were defeated, the Palatinate entirely subdued, and the electorate was conferred upon Maximilian of Bavaria; and the rigid laws against the Protestants were carried into effect in the Palatinate also. It had now become evident to all Europe that the emperor of Austria was determined to stamp out Protestantism throughout Germany; and the Protestant princes, now thoroughly alarmed, besought aid from the Protestant countries, England, Holland and Denmark. King James, who had seen unmoved the misfortunes which had befallen his daughter and her husband, and who had been dead to the general feeling of the country, could no longer resist, and England agreed to supply an annual subsidy; Holland consented to supply troops; and the king of Denmark joined the League, and was to take command of the army.

"In Germany the Protestants of Lower Saxony and Brunswick, and the partisan leader Mansfeldt, were still in arms. The army under the king of Denmark advanced into Brunswick, and was there confronted by that of the League under Tilly; while an Austrian army, raised by Wallenstein, also marched against it. Mansfeldt endeavored to prevent Wallenstein from joining Tilly, but was met and defeated by the former general. Mansfeldt was, however, an enterprising leader, and falling back into Brandenburg, recruited his army, joined the force under the Duke of Saxe-Weimar, and started by forced marches to Silesia and Moravia, to join Bethlem Gabor in Hungary. Wallenstein was therefore obliged to abandon his campaign against the Danes and to follow him. Mansfeldt joined the Hungarian army, but so rapid were his marches that his force had dwindled away to a mere skeleton, and the assistance which it would be to the Hungarians was so small that Bethlem Gabor refused to co-operate with it against Austria.

"Mansfeldt disbanded his remaining soldiers, and two months afterward died. Wallenstein then marched north. In the meantine Tilly had attacked King Christian at Lutter, and completely defeated him. I will tell you about that battle some other time. When Wallenstein came north it was decided that Tilly should carry the war into Holland, and that Wallenstein should deal with the king of Denmark and the Protestant princes. In the course of two years he drove the Danes from Silesia, subdued Brandenburg and Mecklenburg, and, advancing into Pomerania, besieged Stralsund.

"What a siege that was to be sure! Wallenstein had sworn to capture the place, but he didn't reckon upon the Scots. After the siege had begun Lieutenant-general Sir Alexander Leslie, with five thousand Scots and Swedes, fought his way into the town; and though Wallenstein rained fire upon it, though we were half-starved and ravaged by plague, we held out for three months, repulsing every assault, till at last the Imperialists were obliged to draw off, having lost twelve thousand two hundred men.

"This, however, was the solitary success on our side, and a few months since, Christian signed a peace, binding himself to interfere no more in the affairs of Germany. When Ferdinand considered himself free to carry out his plans, he issued an edict by which the Protestants throughout Germany were required to restore to the Catholics all the monasteries and land which had formerly belonged to the Catholic Church. The Catholic service was alone to be performed, and the Catholic princes of the empire were ordered to constrain their subjects, by force if necessary, to conform to the Catholic faith; and it was intimated to the Protestant princes that they would be equally forced to carry the edict into effect. But this was too much. Even France disapproved, not from any feeling of pity on the part of Richelieu for the Protestants, but because it did not suit the interests of France that Ferdinand should become the absolute monarch of all Germany.

"In these circumstances Gustavus of Sweden at once resolved to assist the Protestants in arms, and ere long will take the field. That is what has brought us here. Already in the Swedish army there are ten thousand Scotchmen, and in Denmark they also form the backbone of the force; and both in the Swedish and Danish armies the greater part of the native troops are officered and commanded by Scotchmen.

"Hitherto I myself have been in the Danish service, but my regiment is about to take service with the Swedes. It has been quietly intimated to us that there will be no objection to our doing so, although Christian intends to remain neutral, at any rate for a time. We suffered very heavily at Lutter, and I need five hundred men to fill up my ranks to the full strength.

"Now, Græme, I quite rely upon you. You were at college with Hepburn, Hume, and myself, and it will be a pleasure for us all to fight side by side; and if I know anything of your disposition I am sure you cannot be contented to be remaining here at the age of nine-and-twenty, rusting out your life as a Scotch laird, while Hepburn has already won a name which is known through Europe."

CHAPTER II.

SHIPWRECKED.

Upon the following morning Nigel Græme told his visitors that he had determined to accept their offer, and would at once set to work to raise a company.

"I have," he said, "as you know, a small patrimony of my own, and as for the last eight years I have been living here looking after Malcolm I have been laying by my rents, and can now furnish the arms and accouterments for a hundred men without difficulty. When Malcolm comes of age he must act for himself, and can raise two or three hundred men if he chooses; but at present he will march in my company. I understand that I have the appointment of my own officers."

"Yes, until you join the regiment," Munro said. "You have the first appointments. Afterward the colonel will fill up vacancies. You must decide how you will arm your men, for you must know that Gustavus' regiments have their right and left wings composed of musketeers, while the center is formed of pikemen, so you must decide to which branch your company shall belong."

"I would choose the pike," Nigel said, "for after all it must be by the pike that the battle is decided."

"Quite right, Nigel. I have here with me a drawing of the armor in use with us. You see they have helmets of an acorn shape, with a rim turning up in front; gauntlets, buff-coats well padded in front, and large breastplates. The pikes vary from fourteen to eighteen feet long according to the taste of the commander. We generally use about sixteen. If your company is a hundred strong you will have two lieutenants and three ensigns. Be careful in choosing your officers. I will fill in the king's commission to you as captain of the company, authorizing you to enlist men for his service and to appoint officers thereto."

An hour or two later Colonel Munro and Captain Hume proceeded on their way. The news speedily spread through Nithsdale that Nigel Græme had received a commission from the king of Sweden to raise a company in his service, and very speedily men began to pour in. The disbandment of the Scottish army had left but few careers open at home to the youth of that country, and very large numbers had consequently flocked to the Continent and taken service in one or other of the armies there, any opening of the sort, therefore, had only to be known to be freely embraced. Consequently, in eight-and-forty hours Nigel Græme had applications from a far larger number than he could accept, and he was enabled to pick and choose among the applicants. Many young men of good family were among them, for in those days service in the ranks was regarded as honorable, and great numbers of young men of good family and education trailed a pike in the Scotch regiments in the service of the various powers of Europe. Two young men whose property adjoined his own, Herries and Farquhar, each of whom brought twenty of his own tenants with him, were appointed lieutenants, while two others, Leslie and Jamieson, were with Malcolm named as ensigns. The non-commissioned officers were appointed from men who had served before. Many of the men already possessed armor which was suitable, for in those days there was no strict uniformity of military attire, and the armies of the various nationalities differed very slightly from each other. Colonel Munro returned in the course of a fortnight, Nigel Græme's company completing the number of men required to fill up the ranks of his regiment.

Captain Hume had proceeded further north. Colonel Munro stopped for a week in Nithsdale, giving instructions to the officers and non-commissioned officers as to the drill in use in the Swedish army. Military maneuvers were in these days very different to what they have now become. The movements were few and simple, and easily acquired. Gustavus had, however, introduced an entirely new formation into his army. Hitherto troops had fought in solid masses, twenty or more deep. Gustavus taught his men to fight six deep, maintaining that if troops were steady this depth of formation should be able to sustain any assault upon it, and that with a greater depth the men behind were useless in the fight. His cavalry fought only three deep. The recruits acquired the new tactics with little difficulty. In Scotland for generations every man and boy had received a certain military training, and all were instructed in the use of the pike; consequently, at the end of a week Colonel Munro pronounced Nigel Græme's company capable of taking their place in the regiment without discredit, and so went forward to see to the training of the companies of Hamilton, Balfour, and Scott, having arranged with Græme to march his company to Dunbar in three weeks' time, when he would be joined by the other three companies.

Malcolm was delighted with the stir and bustle of his new life. Accustomed to hard exercise, to climbing and swimming, he was a strong and well-grown lad, and was in appearance fully a year beyond his age. He felt but little fatigued by the incessant drill in which the days were passed, though he was glad enough of an evening to lay aside his armor of which the officers wore in those days considerably more than the soldiers, the mounted officers being still clad in full armor, while those on foot wore back and arm pieces, and often leg pieces, in addition to the helmet and breastplate. They were armed with swords and pistols, and carried besides what were called half-pikes, or pikes some seven feet long. They wore feathers in their helmets, and the armor was of fine quality, and often richly damascened, or inlaid with gold.

Very proud did Malcolm feel as on the appointed day he marched with the company from Nithsdale, with the sun glittering on their arms and a drummer beating the march at their head. They arrived in due course at Dunbar, and were in a few hours joined by the other three companies under Munro himself. The regiment which was now commanded by Lieutenant-colonel Munro had been raised in 1626 by Sir Donald Mackay of Farre and Strathnaver, one thousand five hundred strong, for the service of the king of Denmark. Munro was his cousin, and when Sir Donald went home shortly before, he succeeded to the command of the regiment. They embarked at once on board a ship which Munro had chartered, and were landed in Denmark and marched to Flensberg, where the rest of the regiment was lying.

A fortnight was spent in severe drill, and then orders were received from Oxenstiern, the chancellor of Sweden, to embark the regiment on board two Swedish vessels, the Lillynichol and the Hound. On board the former were the companies of Captains Robert Munro, Hector Munro, Bullion, Nigel Græme, and Hamilton. Colonel Munro sailed in this ship, while Major Sennot commanded the wing of the regiment on board the Hound. The baggage horses and ammunition were in a smaller vessel.

The orders were that they were to land at Wolgast on the southern shore of the Baltic. Scarcely had they set sail than the weather changed, and a sudden tempest burst upon them. Higher and higher grew the wind, and the vessels were separated in the night. The Lillynichol labored heavily in the waves, and the discomfort of the troops, crowded together between decks, was very great. Presently it was discovered that she had made a leak, and that the water was entering fast.

Munro at once called forty-eight soldiers to the pumps. They were relieved every quarter of an hour, and by dint of the greatest exertions barely succeeded in keeping down the water. So heavily did the vessel labor that Munro bore away for Dantzig; but when night came on the storm increased in fury. They were now in shoal water, and the vessel, already half water-logged, became quite unmanageable in the furious waves. Beyond the fact that they were fast drifting on to the Pomeranian coast, they were ignorant of their position.

"This is a rough beginning," Nigel said to his nephew. "We bargained to run the risk of being killed by the Germans, but we did not expect to run the hazard of being drowned. I doubt if the vessel can live till morning. It is only eleven o'clock yet, and in spite of the pumps she is getting lower and lower in the water."

Before Malcolm had time to answer him there was a tremendous crash which threw them off their feet. All below struggled on deck, but nothing could be seen in the darkness saves masses of foam as the waves broke on the rock on which they had struck. There were two more crashes, and then another, even louder and more terrible, and the vessel broke in two parts.

"Come aft all," Colonel Munro shouted; "this part of the wreck is fixed."

With great efforts all on board managed to reach the after portion of the vessel, which was wedged among the rocks, and soon afterward the forepart broke up and disappeared. For two hours the sea broke wildly over the ship, and all had to hold on for life.

Malcolm, even in this time of danger, could not but admire the calmness and coolness of his young colonel. He at once set men to work with ropes to drag toward the vessel the floating pieces of wreck which were tossing about in the boiling surf. The masts and yards were hauled alongside, and the colonel instructed the men to make themselves fast to these in case the vessel should go to pieces.

Hour after hour passed, and at last, to the joy of all, daylight appeared. The boats had all been broken to pieces, and Munro now set the men to work to bind the spars and timbers together into a raft. One of the soldiers and a sailor volunteered to try to swim to shore with lines, but both were dashed to pieces.

At one o'clock in the day some natives were seen collecting on the shore, and these presently dragged down a boat and launched it, and with great difficulty rowed out to the ship. A line was thrown to them, and with this they returned to shore, where they made the line fast. The storm was now abating somewhat, and Munro ordered the debarkation to commence.

As many of the troops as could find a place on the raft, or could cling to the ropes fastened on its sides, started first, and by means of the line hauled the raft ashore. A small party then brought it back to the ship, while others manned the boat; and so after a number of trips the whole of the troops and crew were landed, together with all the weapons and armor that could be saved.

From the peasantry Munro now learned that they had been wrecked upon the coast of Rugenwalde, a low-lying tract of country in the north of Pomerania. The forts upon it were all in the possession of the Imperialists, while the nearest post of the Swedes was eighty miles away.

The position was not a pleasant one. Many of the arms had been lost, and the gunpowder was of course destroyed. The men were exhausted and worn out with their long struggle with the tempest. They were without food, and might at any moment be attacked by their enemies.

"Something must be done, and that quickly," Munro said, "or our fate will be well-nigh as bad as that of the Sinclairs; but before night we can do nothing, and we must hope that the Germans will not discover us till then."

Thereupon he ordered all the men to lie down under shelter of the bushes on the slopes facing the shore, and on no account to show themselves on the higher ground. Then he sent a Walloon officer of the regiment to the Pomeranian seneschal of the old castle of Rugenwalde which belonged to Bogislaus IV., Duke of Pomerania, to inform him that a body of Scotch troops in the service of the Swedish king had been cast on the coast, and begging him to supply them with a few muskets, some dry powder, and bullets, promising if he would do so that the Scotch would clear the town of its Imperial garrison.

The castle itself, which was a very old feudal building, was held only by the retainers of the duke, and the seneschal at once complied with Munro's request, for the Duke of Pomerania, his master, although nominally an ally of the Imperialists, had been deprived of all authority by them, and the feelings of his subjects were entirely with the Swedes.

Fifty old muskets, some ammunition and some food were sent out by a secret passage to the Scots. There was great satisfaction among the men when these supplies arrived. The muskets which had been brought ashore were cleaned up and loaded, and the feeling that they were no longer in a position to fall helplessly into the hands of any foe who might discover them, restored the spirits of the troops, and fatigue and hunger were forgotten as they looked forward to striking a blow at the enemy.

"What did the colonel mean by saying that our position was well-nigh as bad as that of the Sinclairs?" Malcolm asked Captain Hector Munro, who with two or three other officers was sheltering under a thick clump of bushes.

"That was a bad business," Captain Munro replied. "It happened now nigh twenty years ago. Colonel Monkhoven, a Swedish officer, had enlisted two thousand three hundred men in Scotland for service with Gustavus, and sailed with them and with a regiment nine hundred strong raised by Sinclair entirely of his own clan and name. Sweden was at war with Denmark, and Stockholm was invested by the Danish fleet when Monkhoven arrived with his ships. Finding that he was unable to land, he sailed north, landed at Trondheim, and marching over the Norwegian Alps reached Stockholm in safety, where the appearance of his reinforcements discouraged the Danes and enabled Gustavus to raise the siege.

"Unfortunately Colonel Sinclair's regiment had not kept with Monkhoven, it being thought better that they should march by different routes so as to distract the attention of the Norwegians, who were bitterly hostile. The Sinclairs were attacked several times, but beat off their assailants; when passing, however, through the tremendous gorge of Kringellen, the peasantry of the whole surrounding country gathered in the mountains. The road wound along on one side of the gorge. So steep was the hill that the path was cut in solid rock which rose almost precipitously on one side, while far below at their feet rushed a rapid torrent. As the Sinclairs were marching along through this rocky gorge a tremendous fire was opened upon them from the pine forests above, while hugh rocks and stones came bounding down the precipice.

"The Sinclairs strove in vain to climb the mountain side and get at their foes. It was impossible, and they were simply slaughtered where they stood, only one man of the whole regiment escaping to tell the story."

"That was a terrible massacre indeed," Malcolm said. "I have read of a good many surprises and slaughters in our Scottish history, but never of such complete destruction as that only one man out of nine hundred should escape. And was the slaughter never avenged?"

"No," Munro replied. "We Scots would gladly march north and repay these savage peasants for the massacre of our countrymen, but the king of Sweden has had plenty of occupation for his Scotchmen in his own wars. What with the Russians and the Poles and the Danes his hands have been pretty full from that day to this, and indeed an expedition against the Norsemen is one which would bring more fatigue and labor than profit. The peasants would seek shelter in their forests and mountains, and march as we would we should never see them, save when they fell upon us with advantage in some defile."

At nightfall the troops were mustered, and, led by the men who had brought the arms, they passed by the secret passage into the castle, and thence sallied suddenly into the town below. There they fell upon a patrol of Imperial cavalry, who were all shot down before they had time to draw their swords. Then scattering through the town, the whole squadron of cuirassiers who garrisoned it were either killed or taken prisoners. This easy conquest achieved, the first care of Munro was to feed his troops. These were then armed from the stores in the town, and a strong guard being placed lest they should be attacked by the Austrian force, which was, they learned, lying but seven miles away, on the other side of the river, the troops lay down to snatch a few hours of needed rest.

In the morning the country was scoured, and a few detached posts of the Austrians captured. The main body then advanced and blew up the bridge across the river. Five days later an order came from Oxenstiern, to whom Munro had at once despatched the news of his capture of Rugenwalde, ordering him to hold it to the last, the position being a very valuable one, as opening an entrance into Pomerania.

The passage of the river was protected by entrenchments, strong redoubts were thrown up round Rugenwalde, and parties crossing the river in boats collected provisions and stores from the country to the very gates of Dantzig. The Austrians rapidly closed in upon all sides, and for nine weeks a constant series of skirmishes were maintained with them.

At the end of that time Sir John Hepburn arrived from Spruce, having pushed forward by order of Oxenstiern by forced marches to their relief. Loud and hearty was the cheering when the two Scotch regiments united, and the friends, Munro and Hepburn, clasped hands. Not only had they been at college together, but they had, after leaving St. Andrew's, traveled in companionship on the Continent for two or three years before taking service, Munro entering that of France, while Hepburn joined Sir Andrew Gray as a volunteer when he led a band to succor the Prince Palatine at the commencement of the war.

"I have another old friend in my regiment, Hepburn," the colonel said after the first greeting was over—" Nigel Græme; of course you remember him."

"Certainly I do," Hepburn exclaimed cordially, "and right glad will I be to see him again; but I thought your regiment was entirely from the north."

"It was originally," Munro said; but I have filled up the gaps with men from Nithsdale and the south. I was pressed for time, and our glens of Farre and Strathnaver had already been cleared of all their best men. The other companies are all commanded by men who were with us at St. Andrew's—Balfour, George Hamilton, and James Scott."

"That is well," Hepburn said. "Whether from the north or south, Scots fight equally well; and with Gustavus 'tis like being in our own country, so large a proportion are we of his majesty's army.

And now, Munro, I fear that I must supersede you in command, being senior to you in the service, and having, moreover, his majesty's commission as governor of the town and district."

"There is no one to whom I would more willingly resign the command. I have seen some hard fighting, but have yet my name to win; while you, though still only a colonel, are famous throughout Europe."

"Thanks to my men rather than to myself," Hepburn said, "though, indeed, mine is no better than the other Scottish regiments in the king's service; but we have had luck, and in war, you know, luck is everything."

There were many officers in both regiments who were old friends and acquaintances, and there was much feasting that night in the Scotch camp. In the morning work began again. The peasants of the district, eight thousand strong, were mustered and divided into companies, armed and disciplined, and with these and the two Scotch regiments Hepburn advanced through Pomerania to the gates of Colberg, fifty miles away, clearing the country of the Austrians, who offered, indeed, but a faint resistance.

The Lord of Kniphausen, a general in the Swedish service, now arrived with some Swedish troops, and prepared to besiege the town. The rest of Munro's regiment accompanied him, having arrived safely at their destination, and the whole were ordered to aid in the investment of Colberg, while Hepburn was to seize the town and castle of Schiefelbrune, five miles distant, and there to check the advance of the Imperialists, who were moving forward in strength toward it.

Hepburn performed his mission with a party of cavalry, and reported that although the castle was dilapidated it was a place of strength, and that it could be held by a resolute garrison; whereupon Munro with five hundred men of his regiment was ordered to occupy it. Nigel Græme's company was one of those which marched forward on the 6th of November, and entering the town, which was almost deserted by its inhabitants, set to work to prepare it for defense. Ramparts of earth and stockades were hastily thrown up, and the gates were backed by piles of rubbish to prevent them being blown in by petards.

Scarcely were the preparations completed before the enemy were seen moving down the hillside.

"How many are there of them, think you?" Malcolm asked Lieutenant Farquhar.

"I am not skilled in judging numbers, Malcolm, but I should say that there must be fully five thousand."

There were indeed eight thousand Imperialists approaching, led by the Count of Montecuculi, a distinguished Italian officer, who had with him the regiments of Coloredo, Isslani, Goetz, Sparre, and Charles Wallenstein, with a large force of mounted Croats.

Munro's orders were to hold the town as long as

he could, and afterward to defend the castle to the last man. The Imperial general sent in a message requesting him to treat for the surrender of the place; but Munro replied simply, that as no allusion to the word treaty was contained in his instructions he should defend the place to the last. The first advance of the Imperialists was made by the cavalry covered by one thousand musketeers, but these were repulsed without much difficulty by the Scottish fire.

The whole force then advanced to the attack with great resolution. Desperately the Highlanders defended the town, again and again the Imperialists were repulsed from the slight rampart, and when at last they won their way into the place by dint of numbers, every street, lane, alley, and house was defended to the last. Malcolm was almost bewildered at the din, the incessant roll of musketry, the hoarse shouts of the contending troops, the rattling of the guns, and the shrieks of pain.

Every time the Imperialists tried to force their way in heavy columns up the streets the Scots poured out from the houses to resist them, and meeting them pike to pike hurled them backward. Malcolm tried to keep cool, and to imitate the behavior of his senior officers, repeating their orders, and seeing that they were carried out.

Time after time the Austrians attempted to carry the place, and were always hurled back, although outnumbering the Scots by nigh twenty to one. At last the town was in ruins, and was on fire in a score of places. Its streets and lanes were heaped with dead, and it was no longer tenable. Munro therefore gave orders that the houses should everywhere be set on fire, and the troops fall back to the castle.

Steadily and in good order his commands were carried out, and with leveled pikes, still facing the enemy, the troops retired into the castle. The Imperial general, seeing how heavy had been his losses in carrying the open town, shrank from the prospect of assaulting a castle defended by such troops, and when night fell he quietly marched away with the force under his command.

CHAPTER III.

SIR JOHN HEPBURN.

MUNRO'S first care, when he found that the Imperialists had retreated in the direction of Colberg, was to send out some horsemen to discover whether the Swedes were in a position to cover that town. The men returned in two hours with the report that Field-marshal Horn, with the Swedish troops from Stettin, had joined Kniphausen and Hepburn, and were guarding the passage between the enemy and Colberg.

Two days later a message arrived to the effect that Sir Donald Mackay, who had now been created Lord Reay, had arrived to take the command of his regiment, and that Nigel Græme's company was to march and join him; while Munro with the rest of his command was to continue to hold the Castle of Schiefelbrune.

Shortly afterward General Bauditzen arrived with four thousand men and eighteen pieces of cannon to press the siege of Colberg, which was one of the strongest fortresses in North Germany. On the 13th of November the news arrived that Montecuculi was again advancing to raise the siege; and Lord

Reay with his half-regiment, Hepburn with half his regiment, and a regiment of Swedish infantry marched out to meet him, Kniphausen being in command. They took up a position in a little village a few miles from the town; and here, at four o'clock in the morning, they were attacked by the Imperialists, seven thousand strong. The Swedish infantry fled almost without firing a shot, but the Scottish musketeers of Hepburn and Reay stood their ground.

For a time a desperate conflict raged. In the darkness it was utterly impossible to distinguish friend from foe, and numbers on both sides were mown down by the volleys of their own party. In the streets and gardens of the little village men fought desperately with pikes and clubbed muskets. Unable to act in the darkness, and losing many men from the storm of bullets which swept over the village, the Swedish cavalry who had accompanied the column turned and fled; and being unable to resist so vast a superiority of force, Kniphausen gave the word, and the Scotch fell slowly back under cover of the heavy mist which rose with the first breath of day, leaving five hundred men, nearly half their force, dead behind them.

Nigel Græme's company had suffered severely; he himself was badly wounded. A lieutenant and one of the ensigns were killed, with thirty of the men, and many others were wounded with pike or bullet. Malcolm had had his share of the fighting. Several times he and the men immediately round him had been charged by the Imperialists, but their long pikes had each time repulsed the assaults.

Malcolm had before this come to the conclusion, from the anecdotes he heard from the officers who had served through several campaigns, that the first quality of an officer is coolness, and that this is even more valuable than is reckless bravery. He had therefore set before himself that his first duty in action was to be perfectly calm, to speak without hurry or excitement in a quiet and natural tone.

In his first fight at Schiefelbrune he had endeavored to carry this out, but although he gained much commendation from Nigel and the other officers of the company for his coolness on that occasion, he had by no means satisfied himself; but upon the present occasion he succeeded much better in keeping his natural feelings in check, forcing himself to speak in a quiet and deliberate way without flurry or excitement, and in a tone of voice in no way raised above the ordinary. The effect had been excellent, and the soldiers, in talking over the affair next day, were loud in their praise of the conduct of the young ensign.

"The lad was as cool as an old soldier," one of the sergeants said, "and cooler. Just as the Austrian column was coming on for the third time, shouting, and cheering, and sending their bullets in a hail, he said to me as quietly as if he was giving an order about his dinner: 'I think, Donald, it would be as well to keep the men out of fire until the last moment. Some one might get hurt, you

Malcolm's courage and humanity at the battle of Schiefelbrune.—Page 45.
—*The Lion of the North.*

see, before the enemy get close enough to use the pikes.' And then when they came close he said: 'Now, sergeant, I think it is time to move out and stop them.' When they came upon us he was fighting with his half-pike with the best of us. And when the Austrians fell back and began to fire again, and we took shelter behind the houses, he walked about on the road, stooping down over those who had fallen, to see if all were killed, and finding two were alive he called out, 'Will one of you just come and help me carry these men under shelter? They may get hit again if they remain here.' I went out to him, but I can tell you I didn't like it, for the bullets were coming along the road in a shower. His helmet was knocked off by one, and one of the men we were carrying in was struck by two more bullets and killed, and the lad seemed to mind it no more than if it had been a rainstorm in the hills at home. I thought when we left Nithsdale that the captain was in the wrong to make so young a boy an officer, but I don't think so now. Munro himself could not have been cooler. If he lives he will make a great soldier."

The defense of the Scots had been so stubborn that Montecuculi abandoned his attempt to relieve Colberg that day, and so vigilant was the watch which the besiegers kept that he was obliged at last to draw off his troops and leave Colberg to its fate. The place held out to the 26th of February, when the garrison surrendered and were allowed to march out with the honors of war, with pikes carried, colors flying, drums beating, matches lighted, with their baggage, and with two pieces of cannon loaded and ready for action. They were saluted by the army as they marched away to the nearest town held by the Austrians, and as they passed by Schiefelbrune Munro's command were drawn up and presented arms to the fifteen hundred men who had for three months resisted every attempt to capture Colberg by assault.

Nigel Græme's wound was so severe that he was obliged for a time to relinquish the command of his company, which he handed over to Herries.

As there had been two vacancies among the officers Malcolm would naturally have been promoted to the duties of lieutenant, but at his urgent request his uncle chose for the purpose a young gentleman of good family who had fought in the ranks, and had much distinguished himself in both the contests. Two others were also promoted to fill up the vacancies as ensigns.

The troops after the capture of Colberg marched to Stettin, around which town they encamped for a time, while Gustavus completed his preparations for his march into Germany. While a portion of his army had been besieging Colberg, Gustavus had been driving the Imperialists out of the whole of Pomerania. Landing on the 24th of June with an army in all of fifteen thousand infantry, two thousand cavalry, and about three thousand artillery, he had, after despatching troops to aid Munro and besiege Colberg, marched against the

Imperialists under Conti. These, however, retreated in great disorder and with much loss of men, guns, and baggage, into Brandenburg; and in a few weeks after the Swedish landing only Colberg, Greifswald, and Demming held out.

In January Gustavus concluded a treaty with France, who agreed to pay him an annual subsidy of 400,000 thalers on the condition that Gustavus maintained in the field an army of thirty thousand infantry and six thousand cavalry, and assured to the princes and peoples whose territory he might occupy the free exercise of their religion. England also promised a subsidy, and the Marquis of Hamilton was to bring over six thousand intantrny; but as the king did not wish openly to take part in the war this force was not to appear as an English contingent. Another regiment of Highlanders was brought over by Colonel John Munro of Obstell, and also a regiment recruited in the Lowlands by Colonel Sir James Lumsden.

Many other parties of Scotch were brought over by gentlemen of rank. Four chosen Scottish regiments, Hepburn's regiment, Lord Reay's regiment, Sir James Lumsden's musketeers, and Stargate's corps, were formed into one brigade under the command of Hepburn. It was called the Green Brigade, and the doublets, scarfs, feathers, and standards were of that color. The rest of the infantry were divided into the Yellow, Blue, and White Brigades.

One evening when the officers of Reay's regiment

were sitting round the camp-fire Lieutenant Farquhar said to Colonel Munro:

"How is it that Sir John Hepburn has, although still so young, risen to such high honor in the counsel of the king; how did he first make his way?"

"He first entered the force raised by Sir Andrew Gray, who crossed from Leith to Holland, and then uniting with a body of English troops under Sir Horace Vere marched to join the troops of the Elector Palatine. It was a work of danger and difficulty for so small a body of men to march through Germany, and Spinola with a powerful force tried to intercept them. They managed, however, to avoid him, and reached their destination in safety.

"Vere's force consisted of two thousand two hundred men, and when he and Sir Andrew Gray joined the Margrave of Anspach the latter had but four thousand horse and four thousand foot with him. There was a good deal of fighting, and Hepburn so distinguished himself that although then but twenty years old he obtained command of a company of pikemen in Sir Andrew Gray's band, and this company was specially selected as a body-guard for the king.

"There was one Scotchman in the band who vied even with Hepburn in the gallantry of his deeds. He was the son of a burgess of Stirling named Edmund, and on one occasion, laying aside his armor, he swam the Danube at night in front of the Austrian lines, and penetrated to the very heart of the Imperial camp. There he managed to enter the tent of the Imperialist general, the Count de Bucquoi, gagged and bound him, carried him to the river, swam across with him and presented him as a prisoner to the Prince of Orange, under whose command he was then serving.

"It was well for Hepburn that at the battle of Prague he was guarding the king, or he also might have fallen among the hosts who died on that disastrous day. When the elector had fled the country Sir Andrew Gray's bands formed part of Mansfeldt's force, under whom they gained great glory. When driven out of the Palatinate they still kept up the war in various parts of Germany and Alsace. With the Scotch companies of Colonel Henderson they defended Bergen when the Marquis of Spinola besieged it. Morgan with an English brigade was with them, and right steadily they fought. Again and again the Spaniards attempted to storm the place, but after losing twelve thousand men they were forced to withdraw on the approach of Prince Maurice.

"The elector now made peace with the emperor, and Mansfeldt's bands found themselves without employment. Mansfeldt in vain endeavored to obtain employment under one of the powers, but failing, marched into Lorraine. There, it must be owned they plundered and ravaged till they were a terror to the country. At last the Dutch, being sorely pressed by the Spaniards, offered to take them into their pay, and the bands marched out from Lorraine in high spirits.

"They were in sore plight for fighting, for most of them had been obliged to sell even their arms and armor to procure food. Spinola hearing of their approach pushed forward with a strong force to intercept them, and so came upon them at Fleurus, eight miles from Namur, on the 30th of August, 1622.

"The Scots were led by Hepburn, Hume, and Sir James Ramsay; the English by Sir Charles Rich, brother to the Earl of Warwick, Sir James Hays, and others. The odds seemed all in favor of the Spaniards, who were much superior in numbers, and were splendidly accoutered and well-disciplined, and what was more, were well fed, while Mansfeldt's bands were but half armed and almost wholly starving.

"It was a desperate battle, and the Spaniards in the end remained masters of the field, but Mansfeldt with his bands had burst their way through them, and succeeded in crossing into Holland. Here their position was bettered; for, though there was little fighting for them to do, and they could get no pay, they lived and grew fat in free quarters among the Dutch. At last the force broke up altogether; the Germans scattered to their homes, the English crossed the seas, and Hepburn led what remained of Sir Andrew Gray's bands to Sweden, where he offered their services to Gustavus. The Swedish king had already a large number of Scotch in his service, and Hepburn was made a colonel, having a strong regiment composed of his old followers inured to war and hardship, and strengthened by a number of new arrivals.

"When in 1625 hostilities were renewed with Poland Hepburn's regiment formed part of the army which invaded Polish Prussia. The first feat in which he distinguished himself in the service of Sweden was at the relief of Mewe, a town of Eastern Prussia, which was blockaded by King Sigismund at the head of thirty thousand Poles. The town is situate at the confluence of the Bersa with the Vistula, which washes two sides of its walls.

"In front of its other face is a steep green eminence which the Poles had very strongly entrenched, and had erected upon it ten batteries of heavy cannon. As the town could only be approached on this side the difficulties of the relieving force were enormous; but as the relief of the town was a necessity in order to enable Gustavus to carry out the campaign he intended, the king determined to make a desperate effort to effect it.

"He selected three thousand of his best Scottish infantry, among whom was Hepburn's own regiment, and five hundred horse under Colonel Thurn. When they were drawn up he gave them a short address on the desperate nature of the service they were about to perform, namely, to cut a passage over a strongly fortified hill defended by thirty thousand men. The column, commanded by Hepburn, started at dusk, and, unseen by the enemy, approached their position, and working round it began to ascend the hill by a narrow and winding path encumbered by rocks and stones, thick underwood, and overhanging trees.

"The difficulty for troops with heavy muskets, cartridges, breastplates, and helmets, to make their way up such a place was enormous, and the mountain side was so steep that they were frequently obliged to haul themselves up by the branches of the trees; nevertheless, they managed to make their way through the enemy's outposts unobserved, and reached the summit, where the ground was smooth and level.

"Here they fell at once upon the Poles, who were working busily at their trenches, and for a time gained a footing there; but a deadly fire of musketry with showers of arrows and stones, opened upon them from all points, compelled the Scots to recoil from the trenches, when they were instantly attacked by crowds of horsemen in mail-shirts and steel caps. Hepburn drew off his men till they reached a rock on the plateau, and here they made their stand, the musketeers occupying the rock, the pikemen forming in a wall around it.

"They had brought with them the portable chevaux-de-frise carried by the infantry in the Swedish service, they fixed this along in front, and it aided the spearmen greatly in resisting the desperate charges of the Polish horsemen. Hepburn was joined by Colonel Mostyn, an Englishman, and Count Brahe, with two hundred German arquebusiers, and this force for two days withstood the incessant attacks of the whole of the Polish army.

"While this desperate strife was going on, and the attention of the enemy entirely occupied, Gustavus managed to pass a strong force of men and a store of ammunition into the town, and the Poles, seeing that he had achieved his purpose, retired unmolested. In every battle which Gustavus fought Hepburn bore a prominent part. He distinguished himself at the storming of Kesmark and in the defeat of the Poles who were marching to its relief.

"He took part in the siege and capture of Marienburg and in the defeat of the Poles at Dirschau.

"He was with Leslie when last year he defended Stralsund against Wallenstein, and inflicted upon that haughty general the first reverse he had ever met with. Truly Hepburn has won his honors by the edge of the sword."

"Wallenstein is the greatest of the Imperial commanders, is he not?" Farquhar asked.

"He and Tilly," Munro replied. "'Tis a question which is the greatest. They are men of a very different stamp. Tilly is a soldier, and nothing but a soldier, save that he is a fanatic in religion. He is as cruel as he is brave, and as portentously ugly as he is cruel.

"Wallenstein is a very different man. He has enormous ambition and great talent, and his possessions are so vast that he is a dangerous subject for any potentate, even the most powerful. Curiously enough, he was born of Protestant parents, but when they died, while he was yet a child, he was committed to the care of his uncle, Albert Slavata, a Jesuit, and was by him brought up a strict Catholic. When he had finished the course of his study at Metz he spent some time at the University of Altdorf, and afterward studied at Bologna and Padua. He then traveled in Italy, Germany, France, Spain, England and Holland, studying the military forces and tactics of each country.

"On his return to Bohemia he took service under the Emperor Rudolph and joined the army of General Basta in Hungary, where he distinguished himself greatly at the siege of Grau. When peace was made in 1606 Wallenstein returned to Bohemia, and though he was but twenty-three years old he married a wealthy old widow, all of whose large properties came to him at her death eight years afterward.

"Five years later he raised at his own cost two hundred dragoons to support Ferdinand of Gratz in his war against the Venetians. Here he greatly distinguished himself, and was promoted to a colonelcy. He married a second time, and again to one of the richest heiresses of Austria. On the outbreak of the religious war of 1618 he raised a regiment of cuirassiers, and fought at its head. Two years later he was made quartermaster-general of the army, and marched at the head of an independent force into Moravia, and there reestablished the Imperial authority.

"The next year he bought from the Emperor

Ferdinand, for a little over 7,000,000 florins, sixty properties which the emperor had confiscated from Protestants whom he had either executed or banished. He had been made a count at the time of his second marriage; he was now named a prince, which title was changed into that of the Duke of Friedland. They say that his wealth is so vast that he obtains two millions and a half sterling a year from his various estates.

"When in 1625 King Christian of Denmark joined in the war against the emperor, Wallenstein raised at his own cost an army of fifty thousand men and defeated Mansfeldt's army. After that he cleared the Danes out of Silesia, conquered Brandenburg and Mecklenburg, and laid siege to Stralsund, and there broke his teeth against our Scottish pikes. For his services in that war Wallenstein received the duchy of Mecklenburg.

"At present he is in retirement. The conquests which his army have made for the emperor aroused the suspicion and jealousy of the German princes, and it may be that the emperor himself was glad enough of an excuse to humble his to powerful subject. At any rate, Wallenstein's army was disbanded, and he retired to one of his castles. You may be sure we shall hear of him again. Tilly, you know, is the Bavarian commander, and we shall probably encounter him before long."

New Brandenburg and several other towns were captured and strongly garrisoned, six hundred of Reay's regiment under Lieutenant-colonel Lindsay being left in New Brandenburg; Nigel Græme was still laid up, but his company formed part of the force.

"This is ill-fortune indeed," Malcolm said to Lieutenant Farquhar, "thus to be shut up here while the army are marching away to win victories in the field."

"It is indeed, Malcolm, but I suppose that the king thinks that Tilly is likely to try and retake these places, and so to threaten his rear as he marches forward. He would never have placed as strong a force of his best soldiers here if he had not thought the position a very important one."

The troops were quartered in the larger buildings of New Brandenburg; the officers were billeted upon the burghers. The position of the country people and the inhabitants of the towns of Germany during this long and desolating war was terrible; no matter which side won, they suffered. There were in those days no commissariat wagons bringing up stores from depots and magazines to the armies. The troops lived entirely upon the country through which they marched. In exceptional cases, when the military chest happened to be well filled the provisions acquired might be paid for, but as a rule armies upon the march lived by foraging.

The cavalry swept in the flocks and herds from the country round. Flour, forage, and everything else required was seized wherever found, and the unhappy peasants and villagers thought themselves lucky if they escaped with the loss of all they possessed, without violence, insult, and ill treatment. The slightest resistance to the exactions of the lawless foragers excited their fury, and indiscriminate slaughter took place. The march of an army could be followed by burned villages, demolished houses, crops destroyed, and general ruin, havoc, and desolation.

In the cases of towns these generally escaped indiscriminate plunder by sending deputies forward to meet advancing armies, when an offer would be made to the general to supply so much food and to pay so much money on condition that private property was respected. In these cases the main body of the troops was generally encamped outside the town. Along the routes frequently followed by armies the country became a desert, the hapless people forsook their ruined homes, and took refuge in the forests or in the heart of the hills, carrying with them their portable property, and driving before them a cow or two and a few goats.

How great was the general slaughter and destruction may be judged by the fact that the population of Germany decreased by half during the war, and in Bohemia the slaughter was even greater. At the commencement of the war the population of Bohemia consisted of three million of people, inhabiting seven hundred and thirty eight towns and thirty-four thousand seven hundred villages. At the end of the war there were but seven hundred and eighty thousand inhabitants, two hundred and thirty towns, and six thousand villages. Thus three out of four of the whole population had been slaughtered during the struggle.

Malcolm was, with Lieutenant Farquhar, quartered upon one of the principal burghers of New Brandenburg and syndic of the weavers. He received them cordially.

"I am glad," he said, "to entertain two Scottish officers, and, to speak frankly, your presence will be of no slight advantage, for it is only the houses where officers are quartered which can hope to escape from the plunder and exactions of the soldiers. My wife and I will do our best to make you comfortable, but we cannot entertain you as we could have done before this war began, for trade is altogether ruined. None have money wherewith to buy goods. Even when free from the presence of contending armies, the country is infested with parties of deserters or disbanded soldiers, who plunder and murder all whom they meet, so that none dare travel along the roads save in strong parties. I believe that there is scarce a village standing within twenty miles, and many parts have suffered much more than we have. If this war goes on, God help the people, for I know not what will become of them. This is my house, will you please to enter."

Entering a wide hall, he led them into a low sitting-room where his wife and three daughters were at work. They started up with looks of alarm at the clatter of steel in the hall.

"Wife," the syndic said as he entered, "these are two gentlemen, officers of the Scottish regiment; they will stay with us during the occupation of the town. I know that you and the girls will do your best to make their stay pleasant to them."

As the officers removed their helmets the apprehensions of the women calmed down on perceiving that one of their guests was a young man of three or four and twenty, while the other was a lad, and that both had bright pleasant faces in no way answering the terrible reputation gained by the invincible soldiers of the Swedish king.

"I hope," Farquhar said pleasantly, "that you will not put yourselves out of your way for us. We are soldiers of fortune accustomed to sleep on the ground and to live on the roughest fare, and since leaving Scotland we have scarcely slept beneath a roof. We will be as little trouble to you as we can, and our two soldier servants will do all that we need."

Farquhar spoke in German, for so large a number of Germans were serving among the Swedes that the Scottish officers had all learned to speak that language and Swedish, German being absolutely necessary for their intercourse with the country people. This was the more easy as the two languages were akin to each other, and were less broadly separated from English in those days than they are now.

It was nearly a year since Farquhar and Malcolm had landed on the shores of the Baltic, and living as they had done among Swedes and Germans, they had had no difficulty in learning to speak both languages fluently.

CHAPTER IV.

NEW BRANDENBURG.

FARQUHAR and Malcolm Græme were soon at home with their hosts. The syndic had offered to have their meals prepared for them in a separate chamber, but they begged to be allowed to take them with the family, with whom they speedily became intimate.

Three weeks after the capture of New Brandenburg the news came that Tilly with a large army was rapidly approaching.

Every effort was made to place the town in a position of defense. Day after day messengers came in with the news that the other places which had been garrisoned by the Swedes had been captured, and very shortly the Imperialist army was seen approaching. The garrison knew that they could expect no relief from Gustavus, who had ten days before marched northward, and all prepared for a desperate resistance. The townsfolk looked on with trembling apprehension, their sympathies were with the defenders, and, moreover, they knew that in any case they might expect pillage and rapine should the city be taken, for the property of the townspeople when a city was captured was regarded by the soldiery as their lawful prize, whether friendly to the conquerors or the reverse. The town was at once summoned to surrender, and upon Lindsay's refusal the guns were placed in position, and the siege began.

As Tilly was anxious to march away to the north to oppose Gustavus he spared no effort to reduce New Brandenburg as speedily as possible, and his artillery fired night and day to effect breaches in the walls. The Scotch officers saw little of their hosts now, for they were almost continually upon the walls.

At the first news of the approach of the Imperialists the syndic had sent away his daughters to the house of a relative at Stralsund, where his son was settled in business. When Farquhar and Malcolm returned to eat a meal or to throw themselves on their beds to snatch a short sleep, the syndic anxiously questioned them as to the progress of the siege. The reports were not hopeful. In several places the walls were crumbling, and it was probable that a storm would shortly be attempted. The town itself was suffering heavily, for the balls of the besiegers frequently flew high, and came crashing among the houses. Few of the inhabitants were to be seen in the streets; all had buried their most valuable property, and with scared faces awaited the issue of the conflict.

After six days' cannonade the walls were breached in many places, and the Imperialists advanced to the assault. The Scotch defended them with great resolution, and again and again the Imperialists recoiled, unable to burst their way through the lines of pikes or to withstand the heavy musketry fire poured upon them from the walls and buildings.

But Tilly's army was so strong that he was able continually to bring up fresh troops to the attack, while the Scotch were incessantly engaged. For eight-and-forty hours the defenders resisted successfully, but at last, worn out by fatigue, they were unable to withstand the onslaught of the enemy, and the latter forced their way into the town. Still the Scots fought on. Falling back from the breaches, they contested every foot of the ground, holding the streets and lanes with desperate tenacity, and inflicting terrible losses upon the enemy.

At last, twelve hours later, they were gathered in the market place, nearly in the center of the town, surrounded on all sides by the enemy. Several times the Scottish bugles had sounded a parley, but Tilly, furious at the resistance, and at the loss which the capture of the town had entailed, had issued orders that no quarter should be given, and his troops pressed the now diminished band of Scotchmen on all sides.

Even now they could not break through the circle of spears, but from every window and roof commanding them a deadly fire was poured in. Colonel Lindsay was shot dead. Captain Moncrieff, Lieutenant Keith, and Farquhar fell close to Malcolm.

The shouts of "Kill, kill, no quarter," rose from the masses of Imperialists. Parties of the Scotch, preferring to die sword in hand rather than be shot down, flung themselves into the midst of the enemy and died fighting.

At last, when but fifty men remained standing, these in a close body rushed at the enemy and drove them by the fury of their attack some distance down the principal street. Then numbers told. The band was broken up, and a desperate hand-to-hand conflict raged for a time. Two of the Scottish officers alone, Captain Innes and Lieutenant Lumsden, succeeded in breaking their way down a side lane, and thence, rushing to the wall, leaped down into the moat, and swimming across, succeeded in making their escape, and in carrying the news of the massacre to the camp of Gustavus, where the tale filled all with indignation and fury. Among the Scotch regiments deep vows of vengeance were interchanged, and in after-battles the Imperialists had cause bitterly to rue having refused quarter to the Scots at New Brandenburg.

When the last melee was at its thickest, and all hope was at an end, Malcolm, who had been fighting desperately with his half-pike, found himself for a moment in a doorway. He turned the handle, and it opened at once.

The house, like all the others, was full of Imperialists, who had thrown themselves into it when the Scots made their charge, and were now keeping up a fire at them from the upper windows. Closing the door behind him, Malcolm stood for a moment to recover his breath. He had passed unscathed through the three days' fighting, though his armor and helmet were deeply dinted in many places.

The din without and above was tremendous. The stroke of swords on armor, the sharp crack of the pistols, the rattle of musketry, the shouts of the Imperialists, and the wild defiant cries of the Highlanders mingled together.

As Malcolm stood panting he recalled the situation, and, remembering that the syndic's house was in the street behind, he determined to gain it, feeling sure that his host would shelter him if he could. Passing through the house he issued into a courtyard, quickly stripped off his armor and accouterments, and threw them into an out-house. Climbing on the roof of this he got upon the wall, and ran along it until behind the house of the syndic. He had no fear of being observed, for the attention of all in the houses in the street he had left would be directed to the conflict below.

The sound of musketry had already ceased, telling that the work of slaughter was well-nigh over, when Malcolm dropped into the court-yard of the syndic; the latter and his wife gave a cry of astonishment as the lad entered the house, breathless and pale as death.

"Can you shelter me awhile?" he said. "I believe that all my countrymen are killed."

"We will do our best, my lad," the syndic said at once. "But the houses will be ransacked presently from top to bottom."

"Let him have one of the servant's disguises," the wife said; "they can all be trusted."

One of the serving-men was at once called in, and he hurried off with Malcolm.

The young Scotchmen had made themselves very popular with the servants with their courtesy and care to avoid giving unnecessary trouble, and in a few minutes Malcolm was attired as a serving-man, and joined the servants who were busy in spreading the tables with provisions, and generally preparing to ally the passions of the Imperialists.

It was not long before they came. Soon there was a thundering knocking at the door, and upon its being opened a number of soldiers burst in. Many were bleeding from wounds. All bore signs of the desperate strife in which they had been engaged.

"You are welcome," the host said, advancing toward them. "I have made preparations for your coming; eat and drink as it pleases you."

Rushing in, the soldiers fell upon the eatables. Other bands followed, and the house was soon filled from top to bottom with soldiers, who ransacked the cupboards, loaded themselves with such things as they deemed worth carrying away, and wantonly broke and destroyed what they could not. The servants were all kept busy bringing food and drink. This was of good quality, and the soldiers, well satisfied, abstained from personal violence.

All night long pandemonium reigned in the town. Shrieks and cries, oaths and sounds of conflict arose from all quarters, as citizens or their wives were slaughtered by drunken soldiers, or the latter quarreled and fought among themselves for some article of plunder. Flames broke out in many places, and whole streets were burned, many of the drunken soldiers losing their lives in the burning houses; but in the morning the bugles rang out, the soldiers desisted from their orgies, and such as were able to stand staggered away to join their colors.

A fresh party marched into the town; these collected the stragglers, and seized all the horses and carts for the carriage of the baggage and plunder. The burgomaster had been taken before Tilly and commanded to find a considerable sum of money the first thing in the morning, under threat that the whole town would be burned down, and the inhabitants massacred if it was not forthcoming.

A council of the principal inhabitants was hastily summoned at daybreak. The syndics of the various guilds between them contributed the necessary sum either in money or in drafts, and at noon Tilly marched away with his troops, leaving the smoking and ruined town behind him. Many of the inhabitants were forced as drivers to accompany the horses and carts taken away. Among these were three of the syndic's serving-men, Malcolm being one of the number.

It was well that the Pomeranian dialect differed so widely from the Bavarian, so Malcolm's German had consequently passed muster without suspicion. The Imperialist army, although dragging with them an immense train of carts laden with plunder, marched rapidly. The baggage was guarded by horsemen who kept the train in motion, galloping up and down the line, and freely administering blows among their captives whenever a delay or stoppage occurred.

The whole country through which they passed was desolated and wasted, and the army would have fared badly had it not been for the herds of captured cattle they drove along with them, and the wagons laden with provisions taken at New Brandenburg at the other towns they had stormed. The marches were long, for Tilly was anxious to accomplish his object before Gustavus should be aware of the direction he was taking.

This object was the capture of the town of Magdeburg, a large and important city, and one of the strongholds of Protestantism. Here he was resolved to strike a blow which would, he believed, terrify Germany into submission.

When Gustavus heard that Tilly had marched west, he moved against Frankfort on the Oder, where the Imperialists were commanded by Count Shomberg. The latter had taken every measure for the defense of the town, destroying all the suburbs, burning the country houses and mills, and cutting down the orchards and vineyards.

Gustavus, accompanied by Sir John Hepburn, at once reconnoitered the place and posted his troops,

The Blue and Yellow Brigades were posted among the vineyards on the road to Cüstrin; the White Brigade took post opposite one of the two gates of the town. Hepburn and the Green Brigade were stationed opposite the other.

As the Swedes advanced the Imperialist garrison, who were ten thousand strong, opened fire with musketry and cannon from the walls. The weakest point in the defense was assigned by Schomberg to Colonel Walter Butler, who commanded a regiment of Irish musketeers in the Imperialist service. In the evening Hepburn and some other officers accompanied the king to reconnoiter near the walls. A party of Imperialists, seeing some officers approaching, and judging by their waving plumes they were of importance, sallied quietly out of a postern gate unperceived and suddenly opened fire. Lieutenant Munro, of Munro's regiment, was shot in the leg, and Count Teuffel, a colonel of the Life-guards, in the arm. A body of Hepburn's regiment, under Major Sinclair, rushed forward and drove in the Imperialists, a lieutenant-colonel and a captain being captured.

So hotly did they press the Imperialists that they were able to make a lodgment on some high ground near the rampart, on which stood an old churchyard surrounded by a wall, and whence their fire could sweep the enemy's works. Some cannon were at once brought up and placed in position here, and opened fire on the Guben gate. Captain Gunter, of Hepburn's regiment, went forward with twelve men, and in spite of a very heavy fire from the walls, reconnoitered the ditch and approaches to the walls.

The next day all was ready for the assault. It was Palm Sunday, the 3d of April, and the attack was to take place at five o'clock in the afternoon. Before advancing, Hepburn and several of the other officers wished to lay aside their armor, as its weight was great, and would impede their movements. The king, however, forbade them to do so.

"No," he said; "he who loves my service will not risk life lightly. If my officers are killed, who is to command my soldiers?"

Fascines and scaling-ladders were prepared. The Green Brigade were to head the assault, and Gustavus, addressing them, bade them remember New Brandenburg.

At five o'clock a tremendous cannonade was opened on the walls from all the Swedish batteries, and under cover of the smoke the Green Brigade advanced to the assault. From the circle of the walls a cloud of smoke and fire broke out from cannon and arquebus, muskets and wall-pieces. Sir John Hepburn and Colonel Lumsden, side by side, led on their regiments against the Guben gate; both carried petards.

In spite of the tremendous fire poured upon them from the wall they reached the gate, and the two colonels fixed the petards to it and retired a few paces. In a minute there was a tremendous explosion, and the gate fell scattered in fragments.

Then the Scottish pikemen rushed forward. As they did so there was a roar of cannon, and a storm of bullets plowed lanes through the close ranks of the pikemen, for the Imperialists, expecting the attack, had placed cannon, loaded to the muzzle with bullets, behind the gates.

Munro's regiment now leaped into the moat, waded across, and planting their ladders under a murderous fire, stormed the works flanking the gate, and then joined their comrades, who were striving to make an entrance. Hepburn, leading on the pikemen, was hit on the knee, where he had in a former battle been badly wounded.

"Go on, bully Munro," he said jocularly to his old schoolfellow, "for I am wounded."

A major who advanced to take his place at the head of the regiment was shot dead, and so terrible was the fire that even the pikemen of Hepburn's regiment wavered for a moment; but Munro and Lumsden, with their visors down and half-pikes in their hands, cheered on their men, and, side by side, led the way.

"My hearts!" shouted Lumsden, waving his pike —"my brave hearts, let's enter."

"Forward!" shouted Munro; "advance pikes!"

With a wild cheer the Scots burst forward; the gates were stormed, and in a moment the cannon, being seized were turned, and volleys of bullets poured upon the dense masses of the Imperialists. The pikemen pressed forward in close column, shoulder to shoulder, the pikes levelled in front, the musketeers behind firing on the Imperialists in the houses.

In the meantime Gustavus, with the Blue and Yellow Swedish Brigades, stormed that part of the wall defended by Butler with his Irishmen. These fought with extreme bravery, and continued their resistance until almost every man was killed, when the two brigades burst into the town, the White Brigade storming the wall in another quarter.

Twice the Imperialist drums beat a parley, but their sound was deadened by the roar of musketry and the boom of cannon from wall and battery, and the uproar and shouting in every street and house. The Green Brigade, under its commander, maintained its regular order, pressing forward with resistless strength. In vain the Austrians shouted for quarter. They were met by shouts of:

"Remember New Brandenburg!"

Even now, when all was lost, Tilly's verterans fought with extreme bravery and resolution; but at last, when Butler had fallen, and Schomberg and Montecuculi, and a few other officers had succeeded in escaping, all resistance ceased. Four colonels, thirty-six officers, and three thousand men were killed. Fifty colors and ten bagage-waggons, laden with gold and silver plate, were captured.

Many were taken prisoners, and hundreds were drowned in the Oder, across which the survivors of the garrison made their escape. Plundering at once began, and several houses were set on fire; but Gustavus ordered the drums to beat, and the soldiers to repair to their colors outside the town, which was committed to the charge of Sir John Hepburn, with his regiment.

The rumor that Magdeburg was the next object of attack circulated among Tilly's troops the day after they marched west from New Brandenburg. It originated in some chance word dropped by a superior officer, and seemed confirmed by the direction which they were taking, which was directly away from the Swedish army. There was a report, too, that Count Pappenheim, who commanded a separate army, would meet Tilly there, and that every effort would be made to capture the town before Gustavus could march to its assistance.

Malcolm could easily have made his escape the first night after leaving New Brandenburg; but the distance to be traversed to join the Swedish army was great, confusion and disorder reigned everywhere, and he had decided that it would be safer to remain with the Imperialist army until Gustavus should approach within striking distance. On the road he kept with the other two men who had been taken with the horses from the syndic of the weavers, and, chatting with them when the convoy halted, he had not the least fear of being questioned by others. Indeed none of those in the long train of carts and wagons paid much attention to their fellows, all had been alike forced to accompany the Imperialists, and each was too much occupied by the hardships of his own lot, and by thoughts of the home from which he had been torn, to seek for the companionship of his comrades in misfortune.

As soon, however, as Malcolm heard the report of Tilly's intentions, he saw that it was of the utmost importance that the king of Sweden should be informed of the Imperialist plans as early as possible, and he determined at once to start endeavor to make his way across the country. At nightfall the train with the baggage and plunder was as usual so placed that it was surrounded by the camps of the various brigades of the army in order to prevent desertion. The previous night an escape would have been comparatively easy, for the soldiers were worn out by their exertions at the siege of New Brandenburg, and were still heavy from the drink they had obtained there; but discipline was now restored, and the sentries were on the alert. A close cordon of these was placed around the baggage train; and when this was passed, there would still be the difficulty of escaping through the camps of soldiery, and of passing the outposts.

Malcolm waited until the camp became quiet, or rather comparatively quiet, as reveling was still going on in various parts of the camp, for the rigid discipline in use in modern armies was at that time unknown, and except when on duty in the ranks a wide amount of license was permitted to the soldiers. The night was fine and bright, and Malcolm saw that it would be difficult to get through the line of sentries who were stationed some thirty or forty yards apart.

After thinking for some time he went up to a group of eight or ten horses which were fastened by their bridles to a large store-wagon on the outside of the baggage-camp. Malcolm unfastened the bridles and turned the horses' heads outward. Then he gave two of them a sharp prick with his dagger, and the startled animals dashed forward in affright, followed by their companions. They passed close to one of the sentries, who tried in vain to stop them, and then burst into the camp beyond where their rush startled the horses picketed there. These began to kick and struggle desperately to free themselves from their fastenings. The soldiers, startled at the sudden noise, sprang to their feet, and much confusion reigned until the runaway horses were secured and driven back to their lines.

The instant he had thus diverted the attention of the whole line of sentries along that side of the baggage-camp, Malcolm crept quietly up and passed between them. Turning from the direction in which the horses had disturbed the camp, he made his way cautiously along. Only the officers had tents, the men sleeping on the ground around their fires. He had to move with the greatest caution to avoid treading upon the sleepers, and was constantly compelled to make detours to get beyond the range of the fires, round which groups of men were sitting and carousing.

At last he reached the outside of the camp, and

taking advantage of every clump of bushes he had no difficulty in making his way through the outposts, for as the enemy was known to be far away, no great vigilance was observed by the sentries. He had still to be watchful, for fires were blazing in a score of places over the country round, showing that the foragers of the army were at their usual work of rapine, and he might at any moment meet one of these returning laden with spoil.

Once or twice, indeed, he heard the galloping of bodies of horse, and the sound of distant pistol-shots and the shrieks of women came faintly to his ears. He passed on, however, without meeting with any of the foraging parties, and by morning was fifteen miles away from Tilly's camp. Entering a wood he threw himself down and slept soundly for some hours. It was nearly noon before he started again. After an hour's walking he came upon the ruins of a village. Smoke was still curling up from the charred beams and rafters of the cottages, and the destruction had evidently taken place but the day before. The bodies of several men and women lay scattered among the houses; two or three dogs were prowling about, and these growled angrily at the intruder, and would have attacked him had he not flourished a club which he had cut in the woods for self-defense.

Moving about through the village he heard a sound of wild laughter, and going in that direction saw a woman sitting on the ground. In her lap was a dead child pierced through with a lance. The woman was talking and laughing to it, her clothes were torn, and her hair fell in wild disorder over her shoulders. It needed but a glance to tell Malcolm that the poor creature was mad, distraught by the horrors of the previous day.

A peasant stood by leaning on a stick, mournfully regarding her. He turned suddenly round with the weapon uplifted at the sound of Malcolm's approach, but lowered it on seeing that the newcomer was a lad.

"I hoped you were a soldier," the peasant said, as he lowered his stick. "I should like to kill one, and then to be killed myself. My God, what is life worth living for in this unhappy country? Three times since the war began has our village been burned, but each time we were warned of the approach of the plunderers, and escaped in time. Yesterday they came when I was away, and see what they have done;" and he pointed to his wife and child, and to the corpses scattered about.

"It is terrible," Malcolm replied. "I was taken a prisoner but two days since at the sack of New Brandenburg, but I have managed to escape. I am a Scot, and am on my way now to join the army of the Swedes, which will, I hope, soon punish the villains who have done this damage."

"I shall take my wife to her mother," the peasant said, "and leave her there. I hope God will take her soon, and then I will go and take service under the Swedish king, and will slay till I am slain. I would kill myself now, but that I would fain avenge my wife and child on some of these murderers of Tilly's before I die."

Malcolm felt that the case was far beyond any attempt at consolation.

"If you come to the Swedish army ask for Ensign Malcolm Græme of Reay's Scottish regiment, and I will take you to one of the German corps, where you will understand the language of your comrades." So saying he turned from the blood-stained village and continued his way.

CHAPTER V.

MARAUDERS.

MALCOLM had brought with him from Tilly's camp a supply of provisions sufficient for three or four days. Before he started from New Brandenburg the syndic had slipped into his hand a purse containing ten gold pieces, and whenever he came to a village which had escaped the ravages of the war he had no difficulty in obtaining provisions.

It was pitiable at each place the see the anxiety with which the villagers crowded round him upon his arrival and questioned him as to the position of the armies and whether he had met with any parties of raiders on the way. Everywhere the cattle had been driven into the woods; boys were posted as lookouts on eminences at a distance to bring in word should any body of men be seen moving in that direction; and the inhabitants were prepared to fly instantly at the approach of danger.

The news that Tilly's army was marching in the opposite direction was received with a deep sense of thankfulness and relief, for they were now assured of a respite from his plunderers, although still exposed to danger from the arrival of some of the numerous bands. These, nominally fighting for one or other of the parties, were in truth nothing but marauders, being composed of deserters and desperadoes of all kinds, who lived upon the misfortunes of the country, and were even more cruel and pitiless than were the regular troops.

At one of these villages Malcolm exchanged his attire as a serving-man of a rich burgher for that of a peasant lad. He was in ignorance of the present position of the Swedish army, and was making for the entrenched camp of Schwedt, on the Oder, which Gustavus had not left when he had last heard of him.

On the fourth day after leaving the camp of Tilly, as Malcolm was proceeding across a bare and desolate country he heard a sound of galloping behind him, and saw a party of six rough-looking horsemen coming along the road. As flight would have been useless he continued his way until they overtook him. They reined up when they reached him.

"Where are you going, boy, and where do you belong to?" the leader of the party asked.

"I am going in search of work," Malcolm answered. "My village is destroyed and my parents killed."

"Don't tell me that tale," the man said, drawing a pistol from his holster. "I can tell by your speech that you are not a native of these parts."

There was nothing in the appointments of the

men to indicate which party they favored, and Malcolm thought it better to state exactly who he was, for a doubtful answer might be followed by a pistol-shot, which would have brought his career to a close.

"You are right," he said quietly; "but in these times it is not safe always to state one's errand to all comers. I am a Scotch officer in the army of the king of Sweden. I was in New Brandenburg when it was stormed by Tilly. I disguised myself, and, passing unnoticed, was forced to accompany his army as a teamster. The second night I escaped, and am now making my way to Schwedt, where I hope to find the army."

The man replaced his pistol.

"You are an outspoken lad," he said laughing, "and a fearless one. I believe that your story is true, for no German boor would have looked me in the face and answered so quietly; but I have heard that the Scotch scarce know what danger is, though they will find Tilly and Pappenheim very different customers to the Poles."

"Which side do you fight on?" Malcolm asked.

"A frank question and a bold one!" The leader laughed. "What say you, men? Whom are we for just at present? We were for the Imperialists the other day, but now they have marched away, and as it may be the Swedes will be coming in this direction, I fancy that we shall soon find ourselves on the side of the new religion."

The men laughed. "What shall we do with this

boy? To begin with, if he is what he says, no doubt he has some money with him."

Malcolm at once drew out his purse.

"Here are nine gold pieces," he said. "They are all I have, save some small change."

"That is better than nothing," the leader said, pocketing the purse. "And now what shall we do with him?"

"He is a Protestant," one of the men replied; "best shoot him."

"I should say," another said, "that we had best make him our cook. Old Rollo is always grumbling at being kept at the work, and his cooking gets worse and worse. I could not get my jaws into the meat this morning."

A murmur of agreement was raised by the other horsemen.

"So be it," the leader said. "Dost hear, lad? You have the choice whether you will be cook to a band of honorable gentlemen or be shot at once."

"The choice pleases me not," Malcolm replied. "Still, if it must needs be, I would prefer for a time the post of cook to the other alternative."

"And mind you," the leader said sharply, "at the first attempt to escape we string you up to the nearest bough. Carl, do you lead him back and set him to work, and tell the men there to keep a sharp watch upon him."

One of the men turned his horse, and, with Malcolm walking by his side, left the party. They soon turned aside from the road, and after a ride of five miles across a rough and broken country entered a wood. Another half mile and they reached the foot of an eminence, on the summit of which stood a ruined castle.

Several horses were picketed among the trees at the foot of the hill, and two men were sitting near them cleaning their arms. The sight of these deterred Malcolm from carrying into execution the plan which he had formed—namely, to strike down his guard with his club as he dismounted, to leap on his horse, and ride off.

"Who have you there, Carl?" one of the men asked as they rose and approached the newcomers.

"A prisoner," Carl said, "whom the captain has appointed to the honorable office of cook instead of old Rollo, whose food gets harder and tougher every day. You are to keep a sharp eye over the lad, who says he is a Scotch officer of the Swedes, and to shoot him down if he attempts to escape."

"Why, I thought those Scots were very devils to fight," one of the men said, "and this is but a boy. How comes he here?"

"He told the captain his story, and he believed it," Carl said carelessly, "and the captain is not easily taken in. He was captured by Tilly at New Brandenburg, which town we heard yesterday he assaulted and sacked, killing every man of the garrison; but it seems this boy put on a disguise, and being but a boy I suppose passed unnoticed, and was taken off as a teamster with Tilly's army. He gave them the slip, but as he has managed to fall into our hands I don't know that he has gained much by the exchange. Now, youngster, go up to the castle."

Having picketed his horse the man led the way up the steep hill. When they reached the castle Malcolm saw that it was less ruined than it had appeared to be from below. The battlements had indeed crumbled away, and there were cracks and fissures in the upper parts of the walls, but below the walls were still solid and unbroken, and as the rock was almost precipitous, save at the point at which a narrow path wound up to the entrance, it was still capable of making a stout defense against attack.

A strong but roughly made gate, evidently of quite recent make, hung on the hinges, and passing through it Malcolm found himself in the courtyard of the castle. Crossing this he entered with his guide what had once been the principal room of the castle. A good fire blazed in the center; around this half a dozen men were lying on a thick couch of straw. Malcolm's guide repeated the history of the newcomer, and then passed through with him into a smaller apartment, where a man was attending to several saucepans over a fire.

"Rollo," he said, "I bring you a substitute. You have been always grumbling about being told off for the cooking, just because you happened to be the oldest of the band. Here is a lad who will take your place, and to-morrow you can mount your horse and ride with the rest of us."

"And be poisoned, I suppose, with bad food when I return," the man grumbled—"a nice lookout truly."

"There's one thing, you old grumbler, it is quite certain he cannot do worse than you do. My jaws ache now with trying to eat the food you gave us this morning. Another week and you would have starved the whole band to death."

"Very well," the man said surlily; "we will see whether you have gained by the exchange. What does this boy know about cooking?"

"Very little, I am afraid," Malcolm said cheerfully; "but at least I can try. If I must be a cook I will at least do my best to be a good one. Now, what have you got in these pots?"

Rollo grumblingly enumerated their contents, and then putting on his doublet went out to join his comrades in the hall, leaving Malcolm to his new duties.

The latter set to work with a will. He saw that it was best to appear contented with the situation, and to gain as far as possible the good-will of the band by his attention to their wants. In this way their vigilance would become relaxed, and some mode of escape might open itself to him. At dusk the rest of the band returned, and Malcolm found that those who had met him with the captain were but a portion of the party, as three other companies of equal strength arrived at about the same time, the total number mounting up to over thirty.

Malcolm was conscious that the supper was far from being a success; but for this he was not responsible, as the cooking was well advanced when he undertook it; however the band were not dissatisfied, for it was much better than they had been accustomed to, as Malcolm had procured woodwork from the disused part of the castle, and had kept the fire briskly going; whereas his predecessor in the office had been too indolent to get sufficient wood to keep the water on the boil.

In the year which Malcolm had spent in camp he had learned a good deal of rough cookery, for when on active duty the officers had often to shift for themselves, and consequently next day he was able to produce a dinner so far in advance of that to which the band was accustomed that their approbation was warmly and loudly expressed.

The stew was juicy and tender, the roast done to a turn, and the bread, baked on an iron plate, was pronounced to be excellent. The band declared that their new cook was a treasure. Malcolm had already found that though he could move about the castle as he chose, one of the band was now always stationed at the gate with pike and pistols, while at night the door between the room in which he cooked and the hall was closed, and two or three heavy logs thrown against it.

Under the pretense of getting wood Malcolm soon explored the castle. The upper rooms were all roofless and open to the air. There were no windows on the side upon which the path ascended, and by which alone an attack upon the castle was possible. Here the walls were pierced only by narrow loopholes for arrows or musketry. On the other sides the windows were large, for here the steepness of the rock protected the castle from attack.

The kitchen in which he cooked and slept had no other entrance save that into the hall, the doorway into the courtyard being closed by a heap of fallen stones from above. Two or three narrow slits in the wall allowed light and air to enter. Malcolm saw that escape at night, after he had once been shut in, was impossible, and that in the daytime he could not pass out by the gate; for even if by a sudden surprise he overpowered the sentry there, he would be met at the bottom of the path by the two men who were always stationed as guards to the horses, and to give notice of the approach of strangers.

The only chance of escape, therefore, was by lowering himself from one of the windows behind down the steep rock. To do this a rope of some seventy feet long was necessary, and after a careful search through the ruins he failed to discover even the shortest piece of rope.

That afternoon some of the band on their return from foraging drove in half a dozen cattle, and one of these was with much difficulty compelled to climb up the path to the castle, and was slaughtered in the yard.

"There, Scot, are victuals for the next week; cut it up, and throw the head and offal down the rock behind."

As Malcolm commenced his unpleasant task a thought suddenly struck him, and he labored away cheerfully and hopefully. After cutting up the animal into quarters he threw the head, the lower joints of the legs, and the offal from the window. The hide he carried, with the four quarters, into his kitchen, and there concealed it under the pile of straw which served for his bed.

When the dinner was over and the usual carousal had begun, and he knew there was no chance of any of the freebooters coming into the room, he spread out the hide on the floor, cut off the edges, and trimmed it up till it was nearly circular in form, and then began to cut a strip two inches wide round and round till he reached the center. This gave him a thong of over a hundred feet long. Tying one end to a ring in the wall he twisted the long strip until it assumed the form of a rope, which was, he was sure, strong enough to bear many times his weight.

This part of the work was done after the freebooters had retired to rest. When he had finished cutting the hide he went in as usual and sat down with them, as he wished to appear contented with his position. The freebooters were discussing an attack upon a village some thirty miles away. It lay in a secluded position, and had so far escaped pillage either by the armies or wandering bands. The captain said he had learned that the principal farmer was a well-to-do man with a large herd of cattle, some good horses, and a well-stocked house. It was finally agreed that the band should the next day carry out another raid which had already been decided upon, and that they should on the day following that sack and burn Glogau.

As soon as the majority of the band had started in the morning Malcolm made his way with his rope to the back of the castle, fastened it to the window, and launched himself over the rock, which, although too steep to climb, was not perpendicular; and holding by the rope Malcolm had no difficulty in lowering himself down. He had before starting taken a brace of pistols and a sword from the heap of weapons which the freebooters had collected in their raids, and as soon as he reached the ground he struck off through the wood.

Enough had been said during the conversation the night before to indicate the direction in which Glogau lay, and he determined in the first place, to warn the inhabitants of the village of the fate which the freebooters intended for them.

He walked miles before seeing a single person in the deserted fields. He had long since left the wood, and was now traversing the open country, frequently turning round to examine the country around him, for at any moment after he had left, his absence from the castle might be discovered, and the pursuit begun. He hoped, however, that two or three hours at least would elapse before the discovery was made. He had, before starting, piled high the fire in the hall, and had placed plenty of logs for the purpose of replenishing it close at hand.

He put tankards on the board, and with them a large jug full of water, so that the freebooters would have no occasion to call for him, and unless they wanted him they would be unlikely to look into the kitchen.

Except when occasionally breaking into a walk to get breath, he ran steadily on. It was not until he had gone nearly ten miles that he saw a goatherd tending a few goats, and from him he learned the direction of Glogau, and was glad to find he had not gone very far out of the direct line. At last, after asking the way several times, he arrived within a short distance of the village. The ground had now become undulating, and the slopes were covered with trees. The village lay up a valley, and it was evident that the road he was traveling was but little frequented ending probably at the village itself. Proceeding for nearly two miles through a wood he came suddenly upon Glogau.

It stood near the head of the valley, which was here free of trees, and some cultivated fields lay around it. The houses were surrounded by fruit-trees, and an air of peace and tranquillity prevailed such as Malcolm had not seen before since he left his native country. One house was much larger than the rest; several stacks stood in the rick-yard, and the large stables and barns gave a proof of the prosperity of its owner. The war which had already devastated a great part of Germany had passed by this secluded hamlet.

No signs of work were to be seen, the village was

as still and quiet as if it was deserted. Suddenly Malcolm remembered that it was the Sabbath, which, though always kept strictly by the Scotch and Swedish soldiers when in camp, for the most part passed unobserved when they were engaged in active service. Malcolm turned his steps toward the house; as he neared it he heard the sound of singing within. The door was open, and he entered and found himself on the threshold of a large apartment in which some twenty men and twice as many women and children were standing singing a hymn which was led by a venerable pastor who stood at the head of the room, with a powerfully built elderly man, evidently the master of the house, near him.

The singing was not interrupted by the entrance of the newcomer. Many eyes were cast in his direction, but seeing that their leaders went on unmoved, the little congregation continued their hymn with great fervor and force. When they had done the pastor prayed for some time, and then dismissed the congregation with his blessing. They filed out in a quiet and orderly way, but not until the last had left did the master of the house show any sign of observing Malcolm, who had taken his place near the door.

Then he said gravely, "Strangers do not often find their way to Glogau, and in truth we can do without them, for a stranger in these times too often means a foe; but you are young, my lad, though strong enough to bear weapons, and can mean us no ill. What is it that brings you to our quiet village?"

"I have, sir, but this morning escaped from the hands of the freebooters at Wolfsburg, and I come to warn you that last night I heard them agree to attack and sack your village to-morrow; therefore, before pursuing my own way, which is to the camp of the Swedish king, in whose service I am, I came hither to warn you of their intention."

Exclamations of alarm arose from the females of the farmer's family, who were sitting at the end of the room. The farmer waved his hand and the women were instantly silent.

"This is bad news, truly," he said gravely; "hitherto God has protected our village and suffered us to worship Him in our own way in peace and in quiet in spite of the decrees of emperors and princes. This gang of Wolfsburg have long been a scourge to the country around it, and terrible are the tales we have heard of their violence and cruelty. I have for weeks feared that sooner or later they would extend their ravages even to this secluded spot.

"And, indeed, I thank you, brave youth, for the warning you have given us, which will enable us to send our womenkind, our cattle and horses, to a place of safety before these scourges of God arrive here. Gretchen, place food and drink before this youth who has done us so great a service; doubtless he is hungry and thirsty, for 'tis a long journey from Wolfsburg hither."

"What think you, father, shall I warn the men at once of the coming danger, or shall I let them sleep quietly this Sabbath night for the last time in their old homes?"

"What time, think you, will these marauders leave their hold?" the pastor asked Malcolm.

"They will probably start by daybreak," Malcolm said, "seeing that the journey is a long one; but this is not certain, as they may intend to remain here for the night, and to return with their plunder on the following day to the castle.

"But, sir," he went on, turning to the farmer, "surely you will not abandon your home and goods thus tamely to these freebooters. You have here, unless I am mistaken, fully twenty stout men capable of bearing arms; the marauders number but thirty in all, and they always leave at least five to guard the castle and two as sentries over the horses; thus you will not have more than twenty-three to cope with. Had they, as they expected, taken you by surprise, this force would have been ample to put down all resistance here; but as you will be prepared for them, and will, therefore, take them by surprise, it seems to me that you should be able to make a good fight of it, stout men-at-arms though the villains be."

"You speak bodly, sir, for one but a boy in years," the pastor said; "it is lawful, nay it is right to defend one's home against these lawless pillagers and murderers; but as you say, evil though their ways are, these freebooters are stout men-at-arms, and we have heard that they have taken a terrible vengeance on the villages which have ventured to oppose them."

"I am a Scottish officer in the king of Sweden's army," Malcolm said, "and fought at Schiefelbrune and New Brandenburg, and in the fight when the Imperialists tried to relieve Colberg; and having, I hope, done my duty in three such desperate struggles against the Imperialist veterans, I need not shrink from an encounter with these freebooters. If you decide to defend the village I am ready to strike a blow at them, for they have held me captive for five days, and have degraded me by making me cook for them."

A slight titter was heard among the younger females at the indignant tone in which Malcolm spoke of his enforced culinary work.

"And you are truly one of those Scottish soldiers of the Swedish hero who fight so stoutly for the faith, and of whose deeds we have heard so much!" the pastor said. "Truly we are glad to see you. Our prayers have not been wanting night and morning for the success of the champions of the reformed faith. What say you, my friend? Shall we take the advice of this young soldier and venture our lives for the defense of our homes?"

"That will we," the farmer said warmly. "He is used to war, and can give us good advice. As far as strength goes, our men are not wanting. Each has his sword and pike, and there are four or five arquebuses in the village. Yes, if there be a chance of success, even of the slightest, we will do our best as men in defense of our homes."

CHAPTER VI.

THE ATTACK ON THE VILLAGE.

"And now," the farmer said to Malcolm, "what is your advice? That we will fight is settled. When, where and how? This house is strongly built, and we could so strengthen its doors and windows with beams that we might hold out for a long time against them."

"No," Malcolm said, "that would not be my advice. Assuredly we might defend the house; but in that case the rest of the village, the herds and granaries, would fall into their hands. To do any good, we must fight them in the wood on their way hither. But although I hope for a favorable issue, I should strongly advise that you should have the herds and horses driven away. Send off all your more valuable goods in the wagons, with your women and children, to a distance. We shall fight all the better if we know that they are all in safety. Some of the old men and boys will suffice for this work. And now, methinks, you had best summon the men, for there will be work for them to-night."

The bell which was used to call the hands from their work in the fields and woods at sunset soon sounded, and the men in surprise came trooping in at the summons. When they were assembled the farmer told them the news he had heard, and the determination which had been arrived at to defend the village.

After the first movement of alarm caused by the name of the dreaded band of the Wolfsburg had subsided Malcolm was glad to see an expression of stout determination come over the faces of the assemblage, and all declared themselves ready to fight to the last. Four of the elder men were told off at once to superintend the placing of the more movable household goods of the village in wagons, which were to set out at daybreak with the cattle and families.

"Now," Malcolm said, "I want the rest to bring mattocks and shovels and to accompany me along the road. There is one spot which I marked as I came along as being specially suited for defense."

This was about half a mile away, and as darkness had now set in the men lighted torches, and with their implements followed him. At the spot which he had selected there was for the distance of a hundred yards a thick growth of underwood bordering the track on either side. Across the road, at the end of the passage nearest to the farm, Malcolm directed ten of the men to dig a pit twelve feet wide and eight feet deep. The rest of the men he set to work to cut nearly through the trunks of the trees standing nearest the road until they were ready to fall.

Ten trees were so treated, five on either side of the road. Standing, as they did, among the undergrowth, the operation which had been performed on them was invisible to any one passing by. Ropes were now fastened to the upper part of the trees and carried across the road, almost hidden from sight by the foliage which met over the path. When the pit was completed the earth which had been taken from it was scattered in the wood out of sight. Light boughs were then placed over the hole. These were covered with earth and sods trampled down until the break in the road was not perceptible to a casual eye.

This was done by Malcolm himself, as the lightest of the party, the boughs sufficing to bear his weight, although they would give way at once beneath that of a horse. The men all worked with vigor and alacrity as soon as they understood Malcolm's plans. Daylight was breaking when the preparations were completed. Malcolm now divided the party, and told them off to their respective posts. They were sixteen in all, excluding the pastor.

Eight were placed on each side of the road. Those on one side were gathered near the pit which had been dug, those on the other were opposite to the tree which was farthest down the valley. The freebooters were to be allowed to pass along until the foremost fell into the pit. The men stationed there were at once to haul upon the rope attached to the tree near it and to bring it down. Its fall would bar the road and prevent the horsemen from leaping the pit. Those in the rear were, if they heard the crash before the last of the marauders had passed through, to wait until they had closed up, which they were sure to do when the obstacle was reached, and then to fell the tree to bar their retreat.

The instant this was done both parties were to run to other ropes and to bring down the trees upon the horsemen gathered on the road, and were then to fall upon them with axe, pike, and arquebus.

" If it works as well as I expect," Malcolm said, " not one of them will escape from the trap."

Soon after daybreak bowls of milk and trays of bread and meat were brought down to the workers by some of the women. As there was no immediate expectation of attack, the farmer himself, with the pastor, went back to the village to cheer the women before their departure.

" You need not be afraid, wife," the farmer said. "I shall keep to my plans, because when you have once made a plan it is foolish to change it; but I deem not that there is any real need for sending you and the wagons and beasts away. This young Scotch lad seems made for a commander, and truly, if all his countrymen are like himself, I wonder no longer that the Poles and Imperialists have been unable to withstand them. Truly he has constructed a trap from which this band of villains will have but little chance of escape, and I trust that we may slay them without much loss to ourselves. What rejoicings will there not be in the fifty villages when the news comes that their oppressors have been killed! The good God has assuredly sent this youth hither as His instrument in defeating the oppressors, even as He chose the shepherd boy David out of Israel to be the scourge of the Philistines."

By this time all was ready for a start and, having seen the wagons fairly on their way, the farmer returned to the wood, the pastor accompanying the women. Three hours passed before there were any signs of the marauders, and Malcolm began to think that the idea might have occurred to them that he had gone to Glogau, and that they might therefore have postponed their raid upon that village until they could make sure of taking it by surprise, and so capturing all the horses and valuables before the villagers had time to remove them. Glogau was, however, quite out of Malcolm's direct line for the Swedish camp, and it was hardly likely that the freebooters would think that their late captive would go out of his way to warn the village in which he had no interest whatever; indeed they would scarcely be likely to recall the fact that he had been present when they were discussing their proposed expedition against it.

All doubts were, however, set at rest when a boy who had been stationed in a high tree near the edge of the wood ran in with the news that a band of horsemen were riding across the plain, and would be there in a few minutes. Every one fell into his appointed place. The farmer himself took the command of the party on one side of the road, Malcolm of that on the other. Matches were blown and the priming of the arquebuses looked to; then they gathered round the ropes, and listened for the tramp of horses.

Although it was but a few minutes before it came the time seemed long to those waiting; but at last a vague sound was heard, which rapidly rose into a loud trampling of horses. The marauders had been riding quietly until they neared the wood, as speed was no object; but as they wished to take the village by surprise—and it was just possible that they might have been seen approaching—they were now riding rapidly.

Suddenly the earth gave way under the feet of the horses of the captain and his lieutenant, who were riding at the head of the troop, and men and animals disappeared from the sight of those who followed. The two men behind them pulled their horses back on their haunches, and checked them at the edge of the pit into which their leaders had fallen.

As they did so a loud crack was heard, and a great tree came crashing down, falling directly upon them, striking them and their horses to the ground. A loud cry of astonishment and alarm rose from those behind, followed by curses and exclamations of rage. A few seconds after the fall of the tree there was a crash in the rear of the party, and to their astonishment the freebooters saw that another tree had fallen there, and that a barricade of boughs and leaves closed their way behind as in front. Deprived of their leaders, bewildered and alarmed at this strange and unexpected occurrence, the marauders remained irresolute. Two or three of those in front got off their horses and tried to make their way to the assistance of their comrades who were lying crushed under the mass of foliage, and of their leaders in the pit beyond.

But now almost simultaneously two more crashes were heard, and a tree from each side fell upon them. Panic-stricken now the horsemen strove to dash through the underwood, but their progress was arrested, for among the bushes ropes had been fastened from tree to tree; stakes had been driven in, and the bushes interlaced with cords. The trees continued to fall till the portion of the road occupied by the troop was covered by a heap of fallen wood and leaf. Then for the first time the silence in the wood beyond them was broken, the flashes of firearms darted out from the brushwood, and then with a shout a number of men armed with pikes and axes sprang forward to the attack.

A few only of the marauders were in a position to offer any resistance whatever. The greater portion were buried under the mass of foliage. Many had been struck down by the trunks or heavy arms of the trees. All were hampered and confused by the situation in which they found themselves. Under such circumstances it was a massacre rather than a fight. Malcolm, seeing the inability of the freebooters to oppose any formidable resistance, sheathed his sword, and left it to the peasants to avenge the countless murders which the band had committed, and the ruin and misery which they had inflicted upon the country.

In a few minutes all was over. The brigands were shot down, piked or slain by the heavy axes through the openings in their leafy prison. Quarter was neither asked for nor given. The freebooters knew that it would be useless, and died cursing their foes and their own fate in being thus slaughtered like rats in a trap. Two or three of the peasants were wounded by pistol-shots, but this was all the injury that their success cost them.

"The wicked have digged a pit, and they have fallen into it themselves," the farmer said as he approached the spot where Malcolm was standing, some little distance from the scene of slaughter. "Verily the Lord hath delivered them into our hands. I understand, my young friend, why you as a soldier did not aid in the slaughter of these villains. It is your trade to fight in open battle, and you care not to slay your enemies when helpless; but with us it is different. We regard them as wild beasts, without heart or pity, as scourges to be annihilated when we have the chance; just as in winter we slay the wolves who come down to attack our herds."

"I blame you not," Malcolm said. "When men take to the life of wild beasts they must be slain as such. Now my task is done, and I will journey on at once to join my countrymen; but I will give you one piece of advice before I go.

"In the course of a day or two the party left at Wolfsburg will grow uneasy, and two of their number are sure to ride hither to inquire as to the tarrying of the band. Let your men with arquebuses keep watch night and day and shoot them down when they arrive. Were I in your place I would then mount a dozen of your men and let them put on the armor of these dead robbers and ride to Wolfsburg, arriving there about daybreak. If they see you coming they will take you to be the band returning. The two men below you will cut down without difficulty, and there will then be but three or four to deal with in the castle.

"I recommend you to make a complete end of them; and for this reason: if any of the band survive they will join themselves with some other party and will be sure to endeavor to get them to avenge this slaughter; for although these bands have no love for each other, yet they would be ready enough to take up each other's quarrel as against country folk, especially when there is a hope of plunder. Exterminate them, then, and advise your men to keep their secret. Few can have seen the brigands riding hither to-day. When it is found that the band have disappeared the country around will thank God, and will have little curiosity as to how they have gone. You will of course clear the path again and bury their bodies; and were I you I would prepare at once another ambush like that into which they have fallen, and when a second band of marauders comes into this part of the country set a watch night and day. Your men will in future be better armed than hitherto, as each of those freebooters carries a brace of pistols. And now, as I would fain be off as soon as possible, I would ask you to let your men set to work with their axes and cut away the boughs and to get me out a horse. Several of them must have been killed by the falling trees, and some by the fire of the arquebuses; but no doubt there are some uninjured."

In a quarter of an hour a horse was brought up together with the helmet and armor worn by the late captain of the band.

As Malcolm mounted, the men crowded round him and loaded him with thanks and blessings for the danger from which he had delivered them, their wives and families.

When the fugitives had left the village a store of cooked provisions had been left behind for the use of the defenders during the day. As the women could not be fetched back before nightfall, the farmer had despatched a man for some of this food, and the wallets on the saddle were filled with sufficient to last Malcolm for three or four days.

A brace of pistols were placed in the holsters, and with a last farewell to the farmer Malcolm gave the rein to his horse and rode away from the village. He traveled fast now and without fear of interruption. The sight of armed men riding to join one or other of the armies was too common to attract any attention and, avoiding large towns, Malcolm rode unmolested across the plain.

He presently heard the report that the Swedes had captured Frankfort-on-the-Oder, and as he approached that town, after four days' riding, heard that they had moved toward Landsberg. Thither he followed them, and came up to them outside the walls of that place six days after leaving Glogau. The main body of the Swedish army had remained in and around Frankfort, Gustavus having marched against Landsberg with only three thousand two hundred musketeers, twelve pieces of cannon, and a strong body of horse. Hepburn and Reay's Scotch regiments formed part of the column, and Malcolm with delight again saw the green scarfs and banners.

As he rode into the camp of his regiment he was unnoticed by the soldiers until he reached the tents of the officers, before which Colonel Munro was standing talking with several others. On seeing an officer approach in full armor they looked up, and a cry of astonishment broke from them on recognizing Malcolm.

"Is it you, Malcolm Græme, or your wraith?" Munro exclaimed.

"It is I in the flesh, colonel, sound and hearty."

"Why, my dear lad," Munro exclaimed, holding out his hand, "we thought you had fallen at the sack of New Brandenburg. Innes and Lumsden were believed to be the only ones who had escaped."

"I have come through it, nevertheless," Malcolm said; "but it is a long story, colonel, and I would ask you first if the king has learned what Tilly is doing."

"No, he has received no news whatever of him since he heard of the affair at New Brandenburg, and is most anxious lest he should fall upon the army at Frankfort while we are away. Do you know aught about him?"

"Tilly marched west from New Brandenburg," Malcolm said, "and is now besieging Magdeburg."

"This is news indeed," Munro said; "you must come with me at once to the king."

Malcolm followed Colonel Munro to the royal tent, which was but a few hundred yards away. Gustavus had just returned after visiting the advanced lines round the city. On being told that Colonel Munro wished to speak to him on important business, he at once came to the entrance of his tent.

"Allow me to present to you, sire, Malcolm Græme, a very gallant young officer of my regiment. He was at New Brandenburg, and I deemed that he had fallen there; how he escaped I have not yet had time to learn, seeing that he has but now ridden into the camp; but as he is bearer of news of the whereabouts of Tilly and his army, I thought it best to bring him immediately to you."

"Well, sir," Gustavus said anxiously to Malcolm, "what is your news?"

Colonel Munro presents Malcolm to the king.—Page 106.
—*The Lion of the North.*

"Tilly is besieging Magdeburg, sire, with his whole strength."

"Magdeburg!" Gustavus exclaimed incredulously. "Are you sure of your news? I deemed him advancing upon Frankfort."

"Quite sure, sire, for I accompanied his column to within two marches of the city, and there was no secret of his intentions. He started for that town on the very day after he had captured New Brandenburg."

"This is important, indeed," Gustavus said; "follow me," and he turned and entered the tent. Spread out on the table was a large map, which the king at once consulted.

"You see, Colonel Munro, that to relieve Magdeburg I must march through Cüstrin, Berlin, and Spandau, and the first and last are strong fortresses. I can do nothing until the Elector of Brandenburg declares for us, and gives us leave to pass those places, for I dare not march round and leave them in my rear until sure that this weak prince will not take sides with the Imperialists. I will dispatch a messenger to-night to him at Berlin demanding leave to march through his territory to relieve Magdeburg. In the meantime we will finish off with this place, and so be in readiness to march west when his answer arrives. And now, sir," he went on, turning to Malcolm, "please to give me the account of how you escaped first from New Brandenburg, and then from Tilly."

Malcolm related briefly the manner of his escape

from the massacre at New Brandenburg, and how, after accompanying Tilly's army as a teamster for two days, he had made his escape. He then still more briefly related how he had been taken prisoner by a band of freebooters, but had managed to get away from them, and had drawn them into an ambush by peasants, where they had been slain, by which means he had obtained a horse and ridden straight to the army.

Gustavus asked many questions, and elicited many more details than Malcolm had deemed it necessary to give in his first recital.

"You have shown great prudence and forethought," the king said when he had finished, "such as would not be looked for in so young a soldier."

"And he behaved, sire, with distinguished gallantry and coolness at Schiefelbrune, and in the destructive fight outside Colberg," Colonel Munro put in. "By the slaughter on the latter day he would naturally have obtained his promotion, but he begged to be passed over, asserting that it was best that at his age he should remain for a time as an ensign."

"Such modesty is unusual," the king said, "and pleases me; see the next time a step is vacant, colonel, that he has it. Whatever his age, he has shown himself fit to do man's work, and years are no great value in a soldier; why, among all my Scottish regiments I have scarcely a colonel who is yet thirty years old."

Malcolm now returned with Colonel Munro to the regiment, and there had to give a full and minute account of his adventures, and was warmly congratulated by his fellow officers on his good fortune in escaping from the dangers which had beset him. The suit of armor was a handsome one, and had been doubtless stripped off from the body of some knight or noble murdered by the freebooters. The leg-pieces Malcolm laid aside, retaining only a cuirass, back-piece, and helmet, as the full armor was too heavy for service on foot.

Two days later the king gave orders that the assault upon Landsberg was to be made that night. The place was extremely strong, and Gustavus had in his previous campaign twice failed in attempts to capture it. Since that time the Imperialists had been busy in strengthening the fortification, and all the peasantry for ten miles round had been employed in throwing up earthworks; but its principal defense was in the marsh which surrounded it, and which rendered the construction of approaches by besiegers almost impossible. Its importance consisted in the fact that from its great strength its garrison dominated the whole district known as the Mark of Brandenburg. It was the key to Silesia, and guarded the approaches to Pomerania, and its possession was therefore of supreme importance to Gustavus. The garrison consisted of five thousand Imperialist infantry and twelve troops of horse, the whole commanded by Count Gratz. The principal approach to the town was guarded by a strong redoubt armed with numerous artillery.

Colonel Munro had advanced his trenches to within a short distance of this redoubt, and had mounted the twelve pieces of cannon to play upon it, but so solid was the masonry of the fort that their fire produced but little visible effect. Gustavus had brought from Frankfort as guide on the march a blacksmith who was a native of Landsberg, and this man had informed him of a postern gate into the town which would not be likely to be defended, as to reach it it would be necessary to cross a swamp flanked by the advanced redoubt and covered with water.

For two days previous to the assault the troops had been at work cutting bushes and trees, and preparing the materials for constructing a floating causeway across the mud and water. As soon as night fell the men were set to work laying down the causeway, and when this was finished the column advanced to the attack. It consisted of two hundred and fifty pikemen under Colonel Munro, and the same number of dragoons under Colonel Deubattel. Hepburn with one thousand musketeers followed a short distance behind them.

The pikemen led the way and passed along the floating causeway without difficulty, but the causeway swayed and often sank under the feet of the cavalry behind them. These, however, also managed to get across. Their approach was entirely unobserved, and they effected an entrance into the town.

Scarcely had they done so when they came upon a body of three hundred Imperialists who were about to make a sally under Colonel Gratz, son of the governor. The pikemen at once fell upon them. Taken by surprise the Imperialists fought nevertheless stoutly, and eighty of the Scots fell under the fire of their musketry. But the pikemen charged home; Colonel Gratz was killed, with many of his men, and the rest taken prisoners. Hepburn marching on behind heard the din of musketry and pressed forward; before reaching the town he found a place in the swamp sufficiently firm to enable his men to march across it and, turning off, he led his troops between the town and the redoubt, and then attacked the latter in the rear where its defenses were weak, and after three minutes' fighting with its surprised and disheartened garrison the latter surrendered.

The redoubt having fallen, and Munro's men having effected a lodgment in the town, while the retreat on one side was cut off by the force of Gustavus, and on the other by a strong body of cavalry under Marshal Horn, the governor sent a drummer to Colonel Munro to say that he was ready to surrender, and to ask for terms. The drummer was sent to Gustavus, who agreed that the garrison should be allowed to march away with the honors of war, taking their baggage and effects with them.

Accordingly at eight o'clock the Count of Gratz

at the head of his soldiers marched out with colors flying and drums beating, and retired into Silesia. A garrison was placed in Landsberg, and the blacksmith appointed burgomaster of the town. Landsberg fell on the 15th of April, and on the 18th the force marched back to Frankfort.

CHAPTER VII.

A QUIET TIME.

In spite of the urgent entreaties of Gustavus and the pressing peril of Magdeburg, the wavering Duke of Brandenburg could not bring himself to join the Swedes. He delivered Spandau over to them, but would do no more. The Swedish army accordingly marched to Berlin and invested his capital. The duke sent his wife to Gustavus to beseech him to draw off his army and allow him to remain neutral; but Gustavus would not listen to his entreaties, and insisted, as the only condition upon which he would raise the siege, that the duke should ally himself with him, and that the troops of Brandenburg should join his army.

These conditions the duke was obliged to accept, but in the meantime his long hesitation and delay had caused the loss of Magdeburg which, after a gallant defense, was stormed by the troops of Pappenheim and Tilly on the 10th of May. The ferocious Tilly had determined upon a deed which would, he believed, frighten Germany into submission; he ordered that no quarter should be given, and for five days the city was handed over to the troops.

History has no record since the days of Attila of so frightful a massacre. Neither age nor sex was spared, and thirty thousand men, women and children were ruthlessly massacred. The result for a time justified the anticipations of the ferocious leader. The terrible deed sent a shudder of horror and terror through Protestant Germany. It seemed, too, as if the catastrophe might have been averted had the Swedes shown diligence and marched to the relief of the city; for in such a time men were not inclined to discuss how much of the blame rested upon the shoulders of the duke of Brandenburg, who was, in fact, alone responsible for the delay of the Swedes.

Many of the princes and free towns which had hitherto been stanch to the cause of Protestantism, at once hastened to make their peace with the emperor. For a time the sack of Magdeburg greatly strengthened the Imperialist cause. No sooner did the news reach the ears of the duke of Brandenburg than his fears overcame him, and he wrote to Gustavus withdrawing from the treaty he had made, and saying that as Spandau had only been delivered to him in order that he might march to the relief of Magdeburg he was now bound in honor to restore it.

Gustavus at once ordered Spandau to be evacuated by his troops, and again marched with the army against Berlin, which he had but a few days before left. Here he again dictated terms, which the duke was forced to agree to.

The Swedish army now marched to Old Brandenburg, thirty-four miles west of Berlin, and there remained for some time waiting until some expected reinforcements should reach it.

The place was extremely unhealthy and great numbers died from malaria and fever, thirty of Munro's musketeers dying in a single week. During this time the king was negotiating with the elector of Saxony and the landgrave of Hesse. These were the two most powerful of the Protestant princes in that part of Germany, and Tilly resolved to reduce them to obedience before the army of Gustavus was in a position to move forward, for at present his force was too small to enable him to take the field against the united armies of Tilly and Pappenheim.

He first fell upon the landgrave of Hesse, and laid Thüringen waste with fire and sword. Frankenhausen was plundered and burned to the ground. Erfurt saved itself from a similar fate by the payment of a large sum of money, and by engaging to supply great stores of provisions for the use of the Imperial army. The landgrave of Hesse-Cassel was next summoned by Tilly, who threatened to carry fire and sword through his dominions unless he would immediately disband his troops, pay a heavy contribution, and receive the Imperial troops into his cities and fortresses; but the landgrave refused to accept the terms.

Owing to the unhealthiness of the district round Old Brandenburg Gustavus raised his camp there and marched forward to Werben, near the junction of the Elbe with the Havel. He was joined there by his young queen, Maria Eleonora, with a reinforcement of eight thousand men, and by the Marquis of Hamilton with six thousand two hundred, for the most part Scotch, who had been raised by him with the consent of Charles I., to whom the marquis was master of the horse.

Werben was distant but a few miles from Magdeburg, and Pappenheim, who commanded the troops in that neighborhood, seeing that Gustavus was now in a position to take the field against him, sent an urgent message to Tilly for assistance; and the Imperial general, who was on the point of attacking the landgrave of Hesse-Cassel, at once marched with his army and effected a junction with Pappenheim, their combined force being greatly superior to that of Gustavus even after the latter had received his reinforcements.

Malcolm had not accompanied the army in its march from Old Brandenburg. He had been prostrated by fever, and although he shook off the attack it left him so weak and feeble that he was altogether unfit for duty. The army was still lying in its swampy quarters, and the leech who had attended him declared that he could never recover his strength in such an unhealthy air. Nigel Græme, who had now rejoined the regiment cured of his wound, reported the surgeon's opinion to Munro.

"I am not surprised," the colonel said, "and there are many others in the same state; but whither can I send them? The elector of Brandenburg is so fickle and treacherous that he may at any moment turn against us."

"I was speaking to Malcolm," Nigel replied, "and he said that he would, he could go for a time to recruit his health in that village among the hills where he had the fight with the freebooters who made him captive. He said he was sure of a cordial welcome there, and it is but three days' march from here."

"'Tis an out-of-the-way place," Munro said, "and if we move west we shall be still further removed from it. There are Imperial bands everywhere harrying the country unguarded by us, and one of these might at any moment swoop down into that neighborhood."

"That is true; but, after all, it would be better that he should run that risk than sink from weakness as so many have done here after getting through the first attack of fever."

"That is so, Nigel, and if you and Malcolm prefer that risk to the other I will not say you nay; but what is good for him is good for others, and I will ask the surgeon to make me a list of twenty men who are strong enough to journey by easy stages, and who yet absolutely require to get out of this poisonous air to enable them to effect their recovery. We will furnish them with one of the baggage-wagons of the regiment, so that they can ride when they choose. Tell the paymaster to give each man in advance a month's pay, that they may have money to pay for what they need. Horses are scarce, so we can give them but two with the wagon, but that will be sufficient as they will journey slowly. See that a steady and experienced driver is told off with them. They had best start at daybreak to-morrow morning."

At the appointed time the wagon was in readiness, and those who had to accompany Malcolm gathered round, together with many of their comrades who had assembled to wish them God-speed. The pikes and muskets, helmets and breast-pieces were placed in the wagon, and then the feverstricken band formed up before it.

Munro, Nigel, and most of the officers came down to bid farewell to Malcolm and to wish him a speedy return in good health. Then he placed himself at the head of the band and marched off, the wagon following in the rear. Before they had been gone a mile several of the men had been compelled to take their places in the wagon, and by the time three miles had been passed the rest had one by one been forced to give in.

Malcolm was one of the last. He took his seat by the driver, and the now heavily-freighted wagon moved slowly across the country. A store of provisions sufficient for several days had been placed in the wagon, and after proceeding fifteen miles a halt was made at a deserted village and two of the houses in the best condition were taken possession of, Malcolm and the sergeant of the party, a young fellow named Sinclair, occupying the one, and the men taking up their quarters in another.

The next morning the benefit of the change and the removal from the fever-tainted air made itself already apparent. The distance performed on foot was somewhat longer than on the preceding day; the men were in better spirits and marched with a brisker step than that with which they had left the camp. At the end of the fourth day they approached the wood in which the village was situated.

"I will go on ahead," Malcolm said. "Our approach will probably have been seen, and unless they know who we are we may meet with but a rough welcome. Halt the wagon here until one returns with news that you may proceed, for there may be pitfalls in the road."

Malcolm had kept the horse on which he had ridden to Landsberg, and it had been tied behind the wagon. During the last day's march he had been strong enough to ride it. He now dismounted, and taking the bridle over his arm he entered the wood. He examined the road cautiously as he went along. He had gone about half way when the farmer with four of his men armed with pikes suddenly appeared in the road before him.

"Who are you," the farmer asked, "and what would you here?"

"Do you not remember me?" Malcolm said. "It is but three months since I was here."

"Bless me, it is our Scottish friend! Why, lad, I knew you not again, so changed are you. Why, what has happened to you?"

"I have had the fever," Malcolm said, "and have been like to die; but I thought that a change to the pure air of your hills and woods here would set me up. So I have traveled here to ask your hospitality."

By this time the farmer had come up and had grasped Malcolm's hand.

"All that I have is yours," he said warmly. "The lookout saw a wagon coming across the plain with three or four men walking beside it, and he thought that many more were seated in it; so thinking that this might be a ruse of some freebooting band, I had the alarm-bell rung, and prepared to give them a hot reception."

"I have brought some sick comrades with me," Malcolm said. "I have no thought of quartering them on you. That would be nigh as bad as the arrival of a party of marauders, for they are getting strength and will, I warrant you, have keen appetites ere long; but we have brought tents and will pay for all we have."

"Do not talk of payment," the farmer said heartily.

"As long as there is flour in the store-house and bacon on the beams, any Scottish soldier of Gustavus is welcome to it, still more if they be comrades of thine."

"Thanks, indeed," Malcolm replied. "I left them

at the edge of the wood, for I knew not what welcome you might have prepared here; and seeing so many men you might have shot at them before waiting to ask a question."

"That is possible enough," the farmer said, "for indeed we could hardly look for friends. The men are all posted a hundred yards further on."

The farmer ordered one of his men to go on and bring up the wagon, and then with Malcolm walked on to the village. A call that all was right brought out the defenders of the ambush. It had been arranged similarly to that which had been so successful before, except that instead of the pit, several strong ropes had been laid across the road, to be tightened breast-high as soon as an enemy came close to them.

"These are not as good as the pit," the farmer said as they passed them; "but as we have to use the road sometimes we could not keep a pit here which, moreover, might have given way and injured any one from a neighboring village who might be riding hither. We have made a strong stockade of beams among the underwood on either side, so that none could break through into the wood from the path."

"That is good," Malcolm said; "but were I you I would dig a pit across the road some twelve feet wide, and would cover it with a stout door with a catch, so that it would bear wagons crossing, but when the catch is drawn it should rest only on some light supports below and would give way at once if a weight came on it. It would, of course, be covered over with turf. It will take some time to make, but it will add greatly to your safety."

"It shall be done," the farmer said. "Wood is in plenty and some of my men are good carpenters. I will set about it at once."

On arriving at the village Malcolm was cordially welcomed by the farmer's wife and daughters.

The guest chamber was instantly prepared for him and refreshments laid on the table, while the maids, under the direction of the farmer's wife, at once began to cook a bounteous meal in readiness for the arrival of the soldiers. A spot was chosen on some smooth turf under the shade of trees for the erection of the tents, and trusses of clean straw carried there for bedding.

Malcolm as he sat in the cool chamber in the farmhouse felt the change delightful after the hot dusty journey across the plain. There was quite an excitement in the little village when the wagon drove up. The men lifted the arms and baggage from the wagon. The women offered fruit and fresh cool water to the soldiers. There was not only general pleasure throughout the village caused by the novelty of the arrival of the party from the outer world, but a real satisfaction in receiving these men who had fought so bravely against the oppressors of the Protestants of Germany. There was also the feeling that so long as this body of soldiers might remain in the village they would be able to sleep in peace and security, safe from the attacks of any marauding band. The tents were soon pitched by the peasants under the direction of Sergeant Sinclair, straw was laid down in them, and the canvas raised to allow the air to sweep through them.

Very grateful were the weary men for the kindness with which they were received, and even the weakest felt that they should soon recover their strength.

In an hour two men came up from the farm-house carrying a huge pot filled with strong soup. Another brought a great dish of stew. Women carried wooden platters, bowls of stewed fruit, and loaves of bread; and the soldiers, seated upon the grass, fell to with an appetite such as they had not experienced for weeks. With the meal was an abundant supply of the rough but wholesome wine of the country.

To the Scottish soldiers after the hardships they had passed through this secluded valley seemed a perfect paradise. They had nought to do save to eat their meals, to sleep on the turf in the shade, or to wander in the woods and gardens free to pick what fruit they fancied. Under these circumstances they rapidly picked up strength, and in a week after their arrival would hardly have been recognized as the feeble band who had left the Swedish camp at Old Brandenburg.

On Sunday the pastor arrived. He did not live permanently at the village, but ministered to the inhabitants of several villages scattered among the hills, holding services in them by turns, and remaining a few days in each. As the congregation was too large for the room in the farm-house the service was held in the open air. The Scottish soldiers were all present, and joined heartily in the singing, although many of them were ignorant of the language, and sang the words of Scotch hymns to the German tunes.

Even the roughest of them, and those who had been longest away from their native country, were much moved by the service. The hush and stillness, the air of quiet and peace which prevailed, the fervor with which all joined in the simple service, took them back in thought to the days of their youth in quiet Scottish glens, and many a hand was passed hastily across eyes which had not been moistened for many a year.

The armor and arms were now cleaned and polished, and for a short time each day Malcolm exercised the men. The martial appearance and perfect discipline of the Scots struck the villagers with admiration the first time they saw them under arms, and they earnestly begged Malcolm that they might receive from him and Sergeant Sinclair some instruction in drill.

Accordingly every evening when work was done the men of the village were formed up and drilled. Several of the soldiers took their places with them in the ranks in order to aid them by their example. After the drill there was sword and pike exercise, and as most of the men had already some knowledge of the use of arms they made rapid progress, and felt an increased confidence in their power to defend the village against the attacks of any small bands of plunderers.

To Malcolm the time passed delightfully. His kind hosts vied with each other in their efforts to make him comfortable, and it was in vain that he assured them that he no longer needed attention and care. A seat was always placed for him in the coolest nook in the room, fresh grapes and other fruit stood in readiness on a table hard by. The farmer's daughters, busy as they were in their household avocations, were always ready to sit and talk with him when he was indoors, and of an evening to sing him the country melodies.

At the end of a fortnight the men were all fit for duty again, but the hospitable farmer would not hear of their leaving, and as news from time to time reached them from the outer world, and Malcolm learned that there was no chance of any engagement for a time between the hostile armies, he was only too glad to remain.

Another fortnight passed and Malcolm reluctantly gave the word that on the morrow the march must be recommenced. A general feeling of sorrow reigned in the village when it was known that their guests were about to depart, for the Scottish soldiers had made themselves extremely popular. They were ever ready to assist in the labors of the village. They helped to pick the apples from the heavily-laden trees, they assisted to thrash out the corn, and in every way strove to repay their entertainers for the kindness they had shown them.

Of an evening their camp had been the rendezvous of the whole village. There alternately the soldiers and the peasants sang their national songs, and joined in hearty choruses. Many of the villagers played on various instruments; and altogether Glogau had never known such a time of festivity and cheerfulness before.

Late in the evening of the day before they had fixed for their departure the pastor rode into the village.

"I have bad news," he said. "A party of Pappenheim's dragoons, three hundred strong, are raiding in the district on the other side of the hills. A man came in just as I mounted my horse, saying that it was expected they would attack Mansfeld, whose count is a sturdy Protestant. The people were determined to resist to the last, in spite of the fate of Magdeburg and Frankenhausen, but I fear that their chance of success is a small one; but they say they may as well die fighting as be slaughtered in cold blood."

"Is Mansfeld fortified?" Malcolm asked.

"It has a wall," the pastor replied, "but of no great strength. The count's castle, which stands on a rock adjoining it, might defend itself for some time, but I question whether it can withstand Pappenheim's veterans. Mansfeld itself is little more than a village. I should not say it had more than a thousand inhabitants, and can muster at best about two hundred and fifty men capable of bearing arms."

"How far is it from here?" Malcolm asked after a pause.

"Twenty-four miles by the bridle path across the hills."

"When were the Imperialists expected to arrive?"

"They were ten miles away this morning," the pastor replied; "but as they were plundering and burning as they went they will not probably arrive before Mansfeld before the morning. Some of the more timid citizens were leaving, and many were sending away their wives and families."

"Then," Malcolm said, "I will march thither at once. Twenty good soldiers may make all the difference, and although I have, of course, no orders for such an emergency, the king can hardly blame me, even if the worst happens, for striking a blow against the Imperialists here. Will you give me a man," he asked the farmer, "to guide us across the hills?"

"That will I right willingly," the farmer said; "but it seems to me a desperate service to embark in. These townspeople are of little good for fighting, and probably intend only to make a show of resistance in order to procure better terms. The count himself is a brave nobleman, but I fear that the enterprise is a hopeless one."

"Hopeless or not," Malcolm said, "I will undertake it, and will at once put the men under arms. The wagon and horses with the baggage I will leave here till I return, that is if we should ever come back again."

A tap of the drum and the soldiers came running in hastily from various cottages where they were spending their last evening with their village friends, wondering at the sudden summons to arms. As soon as they had fallen in, Malcolm joined them.

"Men," he said, "I am sorry to disturb you on your last evening here, but there is business on hand. A party of Pappenheim's dragoons are about to attack the town of Mansfeld, where the people are of the reformed religion. The siege will begin in the morning, and ere that time we must be there. We have all got fat and lazy, and a little fighting will do us good."

The thought of a coming fray reconciled the men to their departure from their quiet and happy resting-place. Armor was donned, buckles fastened, and arms inspected, and in half an hour, after a cordial adieu from their kind hosts, the detachment marched off, their guide with a lighted torch leading the way. The men were in light marching order, having left everything superfluous behind them in the wagon; and they marched briskly along over hill and through forest without a halt, till at three o'clock in the morning the little town of Mansfeld, with its castle rising above it, was visible before them in the first light of morning.

As they approached the walls a musketoon was

fired, and the alarm-bell of the church instantly rang out. Soon armed men made their appearance on the walls. Fearing that the burghers might fire before waiting to ascertain who were the newcomers, Malcolm halted his band and advanced alone toward the walls.

"Who are you who come in arms to the peaceful town of Mansfeld?" an officer asked from the wall.

"I am an officer of his Swedish majesty, Gustavus, and hearing that the town was threatened with attack by the Imperialists, I have marched hither with my detachment to aid in the defense."

A loud cheer broke from the walls. Not only was the reinforcement a most welcome one, small as it was, for the valor of the Scottish soldiers of the king of Sweden was at that time the talk of all Germany, but the fact that a detachment of these redoubted troops had arrived seemed a proof that the main army of the Swedish king could not be far away. The gates were at once opened, and Malcolm with his band marched into Mansfeld.

CHAPTER VIII.

THE SIEGE OF MANSFELD.

"Will it please your worship at once to repair to the castle?" the leader of the townspeople said. "The count has just sent down to inquire into the reason of the alarm."

"Yes," Malcolm replied, "I will go at once. In the meantime, sir, I pray you to see to the wants of my soldiers, who have taken a long night march and will be none the worse for some refreshment. Hast seen aught of the Imperialists?"

"They are at a village but a mile distant on the other side of the town," the citizen said. "Yesterday we counted eighteen villages in flames, and the peasants who have come in say that numbers have been slain by them."

"There is little mercy to be expected from the butchers of Magdeburg," Malcolm replied; "the only arguments they will listen to are steel and lead, and we will not be sparing of these."

A murmur of assent rang through the townsfolk who had gathered round, and then the burgomaster himself led Malcolm up the ascent to the castle. The news that the newcomers were a party of Scots had already been sent up to the castle, and as Malcolm entered the gateway the count came forward to welcome him.

"You are welcome indeed, fair sir," he said. "It seems almost as if you had arrived from the clouds to our assistance, for we had heard that the Swedish king and his army were encamped around Old Brandenburg."

"His majesty has moved west, I hear," Malcolm said; "but we have been a month away from the camp. My detachment consisted of a body of invalids who came up among the hills to get rid of the fever which was playing such havoc among our ranks. I am glad to say that all are restored, and fit as ever for a meeting with the Imperialists. I heard but yestereven that you were expecting an attack, and have marched all night to be here in time. My party is a small one, but each man can be relied upon, and when it comes to hard fighting, twenty good soldiers may turn the day."

"You are heartily welcome, sir, and I thank you much for coming to our aid. The townspeople are determined to do their best, but most of them have little skill in arms. I have a score or two of old soldiers here in the castle, and had hoped to be able to hold this to the end; but truly I despaired of a successful defense of the town. But enter, I pray you, the countess will be glad to welcome you."

Malcolm accompanied the count to the banquet-hall of the castle. The countess, a gentle and graceful woman, was already there; for indeed but few in Mansfeld had closed an eye that night, for it was possible that the Imperialists might attack without delay. By her side stood her daughter, a girl of about fourteen years old. Malcolm had already stated his name to the count, and the latter now presented him to his wife.

"We have heard so much of the Scottish soldiers," she said as she held out her hand, over which Malcolm bent deeply, "that we have all been curious to see them, little dreaming that a band of them would appear here like good angels in our hour of danger."

"It was a fortunate accident which found me within reach when I heard of the approach of the Imperialists. The names of the Count and Countess of Mansfeld are so well known and so highly esteemed through Protestant Germany that I was sure that the king would approve of my hastening to lend what aid I might to you without orders from him."

"I see you have learned to flatter," the countess said smiling. "This is my daughter Thekla."

"I am glad to see you," the girl said; "but I am a little disappointed. I had thought that the Scots were such big, fierce soldiers, and you are not very big—not so tall as papa; and you do not look fierce at all—not half so fierce as my cousin Caspar, who is but a boy."

"That is very rude, Thekla," her mother said reprovingly, while Malcolm laughed gayly.

"You are quite right, Fräulein Thekla. I know

I do not look very fierce, but I hope when my moustache grows I shall come up more nearly to your expectations. As to my height, I have some years to grow yet, seeing that I am scarce eighteen, and perhaps no older than your cousin."

"Have you recently joined, sir?" the countess asked.

"I have served through the campaign," Malcolm replied, "and have seen some hard knocks given, as you may imagine when I tell you that I was at the siege of New Brandenburg."

"Where your soldiers fought like heroes, and, as I heard, all died sword in hand save two or three officers who managed to escape."

"I was one of the three, countess; but the tale is a long one, and can be told after we have done with the Imperialists. Now, sir," he went on, turning to the count, "I am at your orders, and will take post with my men at any point that you may think fit."

"Before doing that," the count said, "you must join us at breakfast. You must be hungry after your long march, and as I have been all night in my armor I shall do justice to it myself. You will, of course, take up your abode here. As to other matters I have done my best, and the townspeople were yesterday all told off to their places on the walls. I should think it were best that your band were stationed in the market-place as a reserve, they could then move to any point which might be seriously threatened. Should the Imperialists enter the town the citizens have orders to fall back here fighting. All their most valuable goods were sent up here yesterday, together with such of their wives and families as have not taken flight, so that there will be nothing to distract them from their duty."

"That is good," Malcolm said. "The thought that one is fighting for home and family must nerve a man in the defense; but when the enemy once breaks in he would naturally think of home first and hasten away to defend it to the last instead of obeying orders and falling back with his comrades in good order and discipline."

The meal was a cheerful one. Malcolm related more in detail how he and his detachment happened to be so far removed from the army.

Just as the meal came to an end a drum beat in the town and the alarm-bells began to ring. The count and Malcolm sallied out at once to the outer wall, and saw a small party of officers riding from the village occupied by the Imperialists toward the town.

"Let us descend," the count said. "I presume they are going to demand our surrender."

They reached the wall of the town just as the Imperialist officers approached the gate.

"In the name of his majesty the emperor," one of them cried out, "I command you to open the gate and to surrender to his good will and pleasure."

"The smoking villages which I see around me,"

Count Mansfeld replied, "are no hopeful sign of any good will or pleasure on the part of his majesty toward us. As to surrendering, we will die rather. But I am willing to pay a fair ransom for the town if you will draw off your troops and march away."

"Beware, sir!" the officer said. "I have a force here sufficient to compel obedience, and I warn you of the fate which will befall all within these walls if you persist in refusing to admit us."

"I doubt not as to their fate," the count replied; "there are plenty of examples before us of the tender mercy which your master's troops show toward the towns you capture. Once again I offer you a ransom for the town. Name the sum, and if it be in reason such as I and the townspeople can pay, it shall be yours; but open the gates to you we will not."

"Very well," the officer said; "then your blood be on your own heads." And turning his horse he rode with his companions back toward the village.

On their arrival there a bustle was seen to prevail. A hundred horsemen rode off and took post on an eminence near the town, ready to cut off the retreat of any who might try to escape, and to enter the town when the gates were forced open. The other two hundred men advanced on foot in a close body toward the principal gate.

"They will try and blow it open with petards," Malcolm said. "Half of my men are musketeers and good shots, and I will, with your permission, place them on the wall to aid the townsfolk there, for if the gate is blown open and the enemy force their way in it will go hard with us."

The count assented and Malcolm posted his musketeers on the wall, ordering Sergeant Sinclair with the remainder to set to work to erect barricades across the street leading from the gate, so that, in case this were blown in, such a stand might be made against the Imperialists as would give the townspeople time to rally from the walls and to gather there.

The Imperialists heralded their advance by opening fire with pistols and musketoons against the wall, and the defenders at once replied. So heavy was the fire that the head of the column wavered, many of the leading files being at once shot down, but, encouraged by their officers, they rallied, and pushed forward at a run. The fire of the townspeople at once became hurried and irregular, but the Scots picked off their men with steady aim. The leader of the Imperialists, who carried a petard, advanced boldly to the edge of the ditch. The fosse was shallow and contained but little water, and he at once dashed into it and waded across, for the drawbridge had, of course, been raised. He climbed up the bank, and was close to the gate, when Malcolm, leaning far over the wall, discharged his pistol at him. The ball glanced from the steel armor.

Malcolm drew his other pistol and again fired, this time more effectually, for the ball struck between the shoulder and the neck at the junction of the breast and back pieces and passed down into the body of the Austrian who, dropping the petard, fell dead; but a number of his men were close behind him.

"Quick, lads!" Malcolm cried. "Put your strength to this parapet. It is old and rotten. Now, altogether! Shove!"

The soldiers bent their strength against the parapet, while some of the townspeople, thrusting their pikes into the rotten mortar between the stones, prised them up with all their strength. The parapet tottered, and then with a tremendous crash fell, burying five or six of the Imperialists and the petard beneath the ruins.

A shout of exultation rose from the defenders, and the Imperialists at once withdrew at full speed. They halted out of gunshot, and then a number of men were sent back to the village, whence they returned carrying ladders, some of which had been collected the day before from the neighboring villages and others manufactured during the night. The enemy now divided into three parties, which advanced simultaneously against different points of the wall.

Notwithstanding the storm of shot poured upon them as they advanced, they pressed forward until they reached the wall and planted their ladders, and then essayed to climb; but at each point the stormers were stoutly met with pike and sword, while the musketeers from the flanking towers poured their bullets into them.

The troops proved themselves worthy of their reputation, for it was not until more than fifty had fallen that they desisted from the attempt and drew off.

"Now we shall have a respite," Malcolm said. "If there are no more of them in the neighborhood methinks they will retire altogether, but if they have any friends with cannon anywhere within reach they will probably send for them and renew the attack."

The day passed quietly. Parties of horsemen were seen leaving the village to forage and plunder the surrounding country, but the main body remained quietly there. The next day there was still no renewal of the attack, but as the enemy remained in occupation of the village Malcolm guessed that they must be waiting for the arrival of reinforcements. The following afternoon a cloud of dust was seen upon the plain, and presently a column of infantry some four hundred strong, with three cannon, could be made out. The townspeople now wavered in their determination. A few were still for resistance, but the majority held that they could not attempt to withstand an assault by so strong a force, and that it was better to make the best terms they could with the enemy.

A parlementaire was accordingly dispatched to the Imperialists asking what terms would be granted should the place surrender.

"We will grant no terms whatever," the colonel in command of the Imperialists said. "The town is

Malcolm counsels the townspeople of Mansfield to resistance.—Page 139.

—*The Lion of the North.*

at our mercy, and we will do as we will with it and all within it; but tell Count Mansfeld that if he will surrender the castle as well as the town at once, and without striking another blow, his case shall receive favorable consideration."

"That will not do," the count said. "They either guarantee our lives or they do not. I give not up my castle on terms like these, but I will exercise no pressure on the townspeople. If they choose to defend themselves till the last I will fight here with them; if they choose to surrender they can do so; and those who differ from their fellows and put no faith in Tilly's wolves can enter the castle with me."

The principal inhabitants of the town debated the question hotly. Malcolm lost patience with them, and said:

"Are you mad as well as stupid? Do you not see the smoking villages round you? Do you not remember the fate of Magdeburg, New Brandenburg, and the other towns which have made a resistance? You have chosen to resist. It was open to you to have fled when you heard the Imperialists were coming. You could have opened the gates then with some hope at least of your lives; but you decided to resist. You have killed some fifty or sixty of their soldiers. You have repulsed them from a place which they thought to take with scarce an effort. You have compelled them to send for reinforcements and guns. And now you are talking of opening the gates without even obtaining a promise that your lives shall be spared. This is the extremity of folly, and all I can say is, if you take such a step you will well deserve your fate."

Malcolm's indignant address had its effect, and after a short discussion the townspeople again placed themselves at the count's disposal, and said that they would obey his orders.

"I will give no orders," the count said. "My Scottish friend here agrees with me that it is useless to try to defend the town. We might repulse several attacks, but in the end they would surely break in, for the walls are old and weak, and will crumble before their cannon. Were there any hope of relief one would defend them to the last, but as it is it would be but a waste of blood, for many would be slain both in the defense and before they could retreat to the castle; therefore we propose at once to withdraw. We doubt not we can hold the castle. Any who like to remain in their houses and trust to the tender mercy of Tilly's wolves can do so."

There was no more hesitation, and a cannon-ball, the first which the Imperialists had fired, at that moment crashed into a house hard by, and sharpened their decision wonderfully.

"I have no great store of provisions in the castle," the count said, "and although I deem it not likely that we shall have to stand a long siege we must be prepared for it. There are already more than seven hundred of your wives and children there, therefore while half of the force continue to show themselves upon the walls, and so deter the enemy from attempting an assault until they have opened some breaches, let the rest carry up provisions to the castle. Any houses from which the women have fled are at once to be broken open. All that we leave behind the enemy will take, and the less we leave for them the better; therefore all stores and magazines of food and drink must be considered as public property. Let the men at once be divided into two bodies—the one to guard the walls, the other to search for and carry up provisions. They can be changed every three or four hours."

The resolution was taken and carried into effect without delay. Most of the horses and carts in the town had left with the fugitives, those that remained were at once set to work. The carts were laden with large barrels and sacks of flour, while the men carried sides of bacon, kegs of butter, and other portable articles on their heads. The Imperialists, seeing the movement up the steep road to the castle gate, opened fire with their arquebuses, but the defenders of the wall replied so hotly that they were forced to retire out of range. The cannon played steadily all day, and by nightfall two breaches had been effected in the wall and the gate had been battered down.

But by this time an ample store of provisions had been collected in the castle and as the Imperialists were seen to form up for the assault the trumpet was sounded, and at the signal the whole of the defenders of the walls left their posts and fell back to the castle, leaving the deserted town at the mercy of the enemy. The Imperialists raised a shout of triumph as they entered the breaches and found them undefended, and when once assured that the town was deserted they broke their ranks and scattered to plunder.

It was now quite dark, and many of them dragging articles of furniture into the streets made great bonfires to light them at their work of plunder. But they had soon reason to repent having done so, for immediately the flames sprang up and lighted the streets, flashes ran round the battlements of the castle, and a heavy fire was opened into the streets, killing many of the soldiers. Seeing the danger of thus exposing the men to the fire from the castle, the Imperialist commander issued orders at once that all fires should be extinguished, that any one setting fire to a house should be instantly hung, and that no lights were to be lit in the houses whose windows faced the castle.

Foreseeing the possibility of an attack from the castle, the Austrians placed a hundred men at the foot of the road leading up to it, and laid their three cannon loaded to the muzzle to command it.

"Have you not," Malcolm asked the count, "some means of exit from the castle besides the way into the town?"

"Yes," the count said, "there is a footpath down the rock on the other side."

"Then," Malcolm said, "as soon as they are fairly drunk, which will be before midnight, let us fall upon them from the other side. Leave fifty of your oldest men with half a dozen veteran soldiers to defend the gateway against a sudden attack ; with the rest we can issue out, and marching round, enter by the gate and breaches, sweeping the streets as we go, and then uniting, burst through any guard they may have placed to prevent a sortie, and so regain the castle."

The count at once assented. In a short time shouts, songs, the sound of rioting and quarrels, arose from the town, showing that revelry was general. At eleven o'clock the men in the castle were mustered, fifty were told off to the defense with five experienced soldiers, an officer of the count being left in command. The rest sallied through a little door at the back of the castle, and noiselessly descended the steep path. On arriving at the bottom they were divided into three bodies. Malcolm with his Scots and fifty of the townspeople formed one. Count Mansfeld took the command of another, composed of his own soldiers and fifty more of the townspeople. The third consisted of eighty of the best fighting men of the town under their own leaders. These were to enter by the gate, while the other two parties came in by the breaches. The moment the attack began the defenders of the castle were to open as rapid a fire as they could upon the foot of the road so as to occupy the attention of the enemy's force there, and to lead them to anticipate a sortie.

The breach by which Malcolm was to enter was the farthest from the castle. and his command would, therefore, be the last in arriving at its station. When he reached it he ordered the trumpeters who accompanied him to sound, and at the signal the three columns rushed into the town uttering shouts of "Gustavus! Gustavus!"

The Imperialists in the houses near were slaughtered with scarcely any resistance. They were for the most part intoxicated, and such as retained their senses were paralyzed at the sudden attack, and panic-stricken at the shouts, which portended the arrival of a relieving force from the army of the king of Sweden. As the bands pressed forward, slaying all whom they came upon, the resistance became stronger; but the three columns were all headed by parties of pikemen who advanced steadily and in good order, bearing down all opposition, and leaving to those behind them the task of slaying all found in the houses.

Lights flashed from the windows and partly lit up the streets, and the Imperialist officers attempted to rally their men; but the Scottish shouts, "A Hepburn! a Hepburn!" and the sight of their green scarfs added to the terror of the soldiers, who were convinced that the terrible Green Brigade of the king of Sweden was upon them.

Hundreds were cut down after striking scarce a blow in their defense, numbers fled to the walls and leaped over. The panic communicated itself to the party drawn up to repel a sortie. Hearing the yells, screams, and shouts, accompanied by the musketry approaching from three different quarters of the town, while a steady fire from the castle indicated that the defenders there might at any moment sally out upon them, they stood for a time irresolute; but as the heads of the three columns approached they lost heart, quitted their station, and withdrew in a body by a street by which they avoided the approaching columns. On arriving at the spot Malcolm found the guns deserted.

"The town is won now," he said. "I will take my post here with my men in case the Austrians should rally; do you with the rest scatter over the town and complete the work, but bid them keep together in parties of twenty."

The force broke up and scattered through the town in their work of vengeance. House after house was entered and searched, and all who were found there put to the sword; but by this time most of those who were not too drunk to fly had already made for the gates.

In half an hour not an Imperialist was left alive in the town. Then guards were placed at the gate and breaches, and they waited till morning. Not a sign of an Imperialist was to be seen on the plain, and parties sallying out found that they had fled in the utmost disorder. Arms, accouterments, and portions of plunder lay scattered thickly about, and it was clear that in the belief that the Swedish army was on them, the Imperialists had fled panic-stricken, and were now far away. Upward of two hundred bodies were found in the streets and houses.

A huge grave was dug outside the walls, and here the fallen foes were buried. Only three or four of the defenders of the town were killed and a score or so wounded in the whole affair. Although there was little fear of a return, as the Imperialists would probably continue their headlong flight for a long distance, and would then march with all haste to rejoin their main army with the news that a strong Swedish force was at Mansfeld, the count set the townspeople at once to repair the breaches.

The people were overjoyed with their success, and delighted at having preserved their homes from destruction, for they knew that the Imperialists would, if unsuccessful against the castle, have given the town to the flames before retiring. The women and children flocked down to their homes again, and although much furniture had been destroyed and damage done, this was little heeded when so much was saved.

All vied in the expression of gratitude toward Malcolm and his Scots, but Malcolm modestly disclaimed all merit, saying that he and his men had scarcely struck a blow.

"It is not so much the fighting," the count said, "as the example which you set the townsmen, and the spirit which the presence of you and your men diffused among them. Besides, your counsel and support to me have been invaluable; had it not been for you the place would probably have been carried at the first attack, and if not the townspeople would have surrendered when the enemy's reinforcements arrived ; and in that case, with so small a force at my command I could not have hoped to defend the castle successfully. Moreover, the idea of the sortie which has freed us of them and saved the town from destruction was entirely yours. No, my friend, say what you will I feel that I am indebted to you for the safety of my wife and child, and so long as I live I shall be deeply your debtor."

The following day Malcolm with his party marched away. The count had presented him with a suit of magnificent armor, and the countess with a gold chain of great value. Handsome presents were also made to Sergeant Sinclair, who was a cadet of good family, and a purse of gold was given to each of the soldiers, so in high spirits the band marched away over the mountains on their return to the village.

CHAPTER IX.

THE BATTLE OF BREITENFELD.

GREAT joy was manifested as Malcolm's band marched into the village and it was found that they had accomplished the mission on which they went, had saved Mansfeld, and utterly defeated the Imperialists, and had returned in undiminished numbers, although two or three had received wounds more or less serious, principally in the first day's fighting. They only remained one night in the village.

On the following morning the baggage was placed in the wagons with a store of fruit and provisions for their march, and after another hearty adieu the detachment set out in high spirits. After marching for two days they learned that the Swedish army had marched to Werben, and that Tilly's army had followed it there.

After the receipt of this news there was no more loitering; the marches were long and severe, and after making a detour to avoid the Imperialists the detachment entered the royal camp without having met with any adventure on the way. His fellow-officers flocked round Malcolm to congratulate him on his safe return and on his restored health.

"The change has done wonders for you, Malcolm," Nigel Græme said. "Why, when you marched out you were a band of tottering scarecrows, and now your detachment looks as healthy and fresh as if they had but yesterday left Scotland; but come in, the bugle has just sounded to supper, and we are only waiting for the colonel to arrive. He is at present in council with the king with Hepburn and some more. Ah! here he comes."

Munro rode up and leaped from his horse, and after heartily greeting Malcolm led the way into the tent where supper was laid out. Malcolm was glad to see by the faces of his comrades that all had shaken off the disease which had played such havoc among them at Old Brandenburg.

"Is there any chance of a general engagement?" he asked Nigel.

"Not at present," Nigel said. "We are expecting the reinforcements up in a few days. As you see we have fortified the camp too strongly for Tilly to venture to attack us here. Only yesterday he drew up his army and offered us battle; but the odds were too great, and the king will not fight till his reinforcements arrive. Some of the hotter spirits were sorry that he would not accept Tilly's invitation, and I own that I rather gnashed my teeth myself; but I knew that the king was right in not risking the whole cause rashly when a few days will put us in a position to meet the Imperialists on something like equal terms. Is there any news, colonel?" he asked, turning to Munro.

"No news of importance," the colonel replied; "but the king is rather puzzled. A prisoner was taken to-day—one of Pappenheim's horsemen—and he declares that a force of horse and foot have been defeated at Mansfeld by the Swedish army with heavy loss. He avers that he was present at the affair, and arrived in camp with the rest of the beaten force only yesterday. We cannot make it out, as we know that there are no Swedish troops anywhere in that direction."

Malcolm burst into a hearty laugh, to the surprise of his fellow-officers.

"I can explain the matter, colonel," he said. "It was my detachment that had the honor of representing the Swedish army at Mansfeld."

"What on earth do you mean, Malcolm?" the colonel asked.

"Well, sir, as you know I went with a detachment to the village where I had before been well treated, and had earned the gratitude of the people by teaching them how to destroy a party of marauders. After having been there for a month I was on the point of marching, for the men were all perfectly restored to health; and indeed I know I ought to have returned sooner, seeing that the men were fit for service; but as I thought you were still at Old Brandenburg, and could well dispense with our services, I lingered on to the last. But just as I was about to march the news came that a party of Imperialist horse, three hundred strong, was about to attack Mansfeld, a place of whose existence I had never heard; but hearing that its count was a stanch Protestant, and that the inhabitants intended to make a stout defense, I thought that I could not be doing wrong in the service of the king by marching to aid them, the place being but twenty-four miles away across the hills. We got there in time, and aided the townspeople to repulse the first assault. After two days they brought up a reinforcement of four hundred infantry and some cannon. As the place is a small one, with but about two hundred and fifty fighting men of all ages, we deemed it impossible to defend the town, and while they were breaching the walls fell back to the castle. The Imperialists occupied it at sunset, and at night, leaving a party to hold the castle, we sallied out from the other side, and marching round entered by the breaches, and, raising the Swedish war-cry, fell upon the enemy, who were for the most part too drunk to offer any serious resistance. We killed two hundred and fifty of them, and the rest fled in terror, thinking they had the whole Swedish army upon them. The next day I started on my march back here, and though we have not spared speed, it seems that the Imperialists have arrived before us."

A burst of laughter and applause greeted the solution of the mystery.

"You have done well, sir," Munro said cordially, and have rendered a great service not only in the defeat of the Imperialists, but in its consequences here, for the prisoner said that last night five thousand men were marched away from Tilly's army to observe and make head against this supposed Swedish force advancing from the east. When I have done my meal I will go over to the king with the news, for his majesty is greatly puzzled, especially as the prisoner declared that he himself had seen the Scots of the Green Brigade in the van of the column, and had heard the war-cry, 'A Hepburn! A Hepburn!'

"Hepburn himself could make neither head nor tail of it, and was half inclined to believe that this avenging force was led by the ghosts of those who had been slain at New Brandenburg. Whenever we can't account for a thing, we Scots are inclined to believe it's supernatural.

"Now tell me more fully about the affair, Malcolm. By the way, do you know you are a lieutenant? Poor Foulis died of the fever a few days after you left us, and as the king had himself ordered that you were to have the next vacancy, I of course appointed you at once. We must celebrate your promotion tonight."

Malcolm now related fully the incidents of the siege.

"By my faith, Malcolm Graeme," Munro said when he had finished, "you are as lucky as you are brave. Mansfeld is a powerful nobleman, and has large possessions in various parts of Germany and much influence, and the king will be grateful that you have thus rendered him such effective assistance and so bound him to our cause. I believe he has no children."

"He has a daughter," Malcolm said, "a pretty little maid some fourteen years old."

"In faith, Malcolm, 'tis a pity that you and she are not four or five years older. What a match it would be for you, the heiress of Mansfeld; she would be a catch indeed! Well, there's time enough yet, my lad, for there is no saying how long this war will last."

There was a general laugh, and the colonel continued:

"Malcolm has the grace to color, which I am afraid the rest of us have lost long ago. Never mind, Malcolm, there are plenty of Scotch cadets have mended their fortune by means of a rich heiress before now, and I hope there will be many more. I am on the lookout for a wealthy young countess myself, and I don't think there is one here who would not lay aside his armor and sword on such an inducement. And now, gentlemen, as we have all finished, I will leave you while I go across with our young lieutenant to the king. I must tell him to-night, or he will not sleep with wondering over the mystery. We will be back anon and will celebrate in honor of Malcolm Græme's promotion."

Sir John Hepburn was dining with Gustavus, and the meal was just concluded when Colonel Munro was announced.

"Well, my brave Munro, what is it?" the king said heartily, "and whom have you here? The young officer who escaped from New Brandenburg and Tilly, unless I am mistaken."

"It is, sire, but I have to introduce him in a new character to-night, as the leader of your majesty's army who have defeated the Imperialists at Mansfeld."

"Say you so?" exclaimed the king. "Then, though I understand you not, we shall hear a solution of the mystery which has been puzzling us. Sit down, young sir, and expound this riddle to us."

Malcolm repeated the narrative as he had told it to his colonel, and the king expressed his warm satisfaction.

"You will make a great leader some day if you do not get killed in one of these adventures, young sir. Bravery seems to be a common gift of the men of your nation; but you seem to unite with it a surprising prudence and sagacity, and, moreover, this march of yours to Mansfeld show that you do not fear taking responsibility, which is a high and rare quality. You have done good service to the cause, and I thank you, and shall keep my eye upon you in the future."

The next day Malcolm went round the camp, and was surprised at the extensive works which had been erected. Strong ramparts and redoubts had been thrown up round it, faced with stone, and mounted with one hundred and fifty pieces of cannon. In the center stood an inner intrenchment with earthworks and a deep fosse. In this stood the tents of the king and those of his principal officers. The marquis of Hamilton had, Malcolm heard, arrived and gone. He had lost on the march many of the soldiers he had enlisted in England, who had died from eating German bread, which was heavier, darker colored, and more sour than that of their own country. This, however, did not disagree with the Scotch, who were accustomed to black bread.

"I wonder," Malcolm said to Nigel Græme, "that when the king has in face of him a force so superior to his own he should have sent away on detached service the four splendid regiments which they say the marquis brought."

"Well, the fact was," Nigel said laughing, "Hamilton was altogether too grand for us here. We all felt small and mean so long as he remained. Gustavus himself, who is as simple in his tastes as any officer in the army, and who keeps up no ostentatious show, was thrown into the shade by his visitor. Why, had he been the emperor of Germany or the king of France he could not have made a braver show. His table was equipped and furnished with magnificence; his carriages would have created a sensation in Paris; the liveries of his attendants were more splendid than the uniforms of generals; he had forty gentlemen as esquires and pages, and two hundred yeomen, splendidly mounted and armed, rode with him as his bodyguard.

"Altogether he was oppressive; but the Hamiltons have ever been fond of show and finery. So

Gustavus has sent him and his troops away to guard the passages of the Oder and to cover our retreat should we be forced to fall back."

Tilly, finding that the position of Gustavus was too strong to be forced, retired to Wolmirstadt, whence he summoned the elector of Saxony to admit his army into his country, and either to disband the Saxon army or to unite it to his own. Hitherto the elector had held aloof from Gustavus, whom he regarded with jealousy and dislike, and had stood by inactive although the slightest movement of his army would have saved Magdeburg. To disband his troops, however, and to hand over his fortresses to Tilly, would be equivalent to giving up his dominions to the enemy; rather than do this he determined to join Gustavus, and having dispatched Arnheim to treat with the king of Sweden for alliance. he sent a point-blank refusal to Tilly.

The Imperialist general at once marched toward Leipzig, devastating the country as he advanced. Terms were soon arranged between the elector and Gustavus, and on the 3d of September, 1631, the Swedish army crossed the Elbe, and the next day joined the Saxon army at Torgau. By this time Tilly was in front of Leipzig, and immediately on his arrival burned to the ground Halle, a suburb lying beyond the wall, and then summoned the city to surrender.

Alarmed at the sight of the conflagration of Halle, and with the fate of Magdeburg in their minds, the citizens of Leipzig opened their gates at once on promise of fair treatment. The news of this speedy surrender was a heavy blow to the allies, who, however after a council of war, determined at once to march forward against the city, and to give battle to the Imperialists on the plain around it.

Leipzig stands on a wide plain which is called the plain of Breitenfeld, and the battle which was about to commence there has been called by the Germans the battle of Breitenfeld, to distinguish it from the even greater struggles which have since taken place under the walls of Leipzig.

The baggage had all been left behind, and the Swedish army lay down as they stood. The king occupied his traveling coach, and passed the night chatting with Sir John Hepburn, Marshal Horn, Sir John Banner, Baron Teuffel, who commanded the guards, and other leaders. The lines of red fires which marked Tilly's position on the slope of a gentle eminence to the southwest were plainly to be seen. The day broke dull and misty on the 7th of September, and as the light fog gradually rose the troops formed up for battle.

Prayers were said in front of every regiment, and the army then moved forward. Two Scottish brigades had the places of honor in the van, where the regiments of Sir James Ramsay, the laird of Foulis, and Sir John Hamilton were posted, while Hepburn's Green Brigade formed part of the reserve—a force composed of the best troops of the army, as on them the fate of the battle frequently depends. The Swedish cavalry were commanded by

Field-marshal Horn, General Banner, and Lieutenant-general Bauditzen.

The king and Baron Teuffel led the main body of infantry; the king of Saxony commanded the Saxons, who were on the Swedish left. The armies were not very unequal in numbers, the allies numbering thirty-five thousand, of whom the Swedes and Scots counted twenty thousand, the Saxons fifteen thousand. The Imperialists numbered about forty thousand. Tilly was fighting unwillingly, for he had wished to await the arrival from Italy of twelve thousand veterans under General Altringer, and who were within a few days' march; but he had been induced, against his own better judgment, by the urgency of Pappenheim, Fürstenberg, and the younger generals, to quit the unassailable post he had taken up in front of Leipzig, and to move out on to the plain of Breitenfeld to accept the battle which the Swedes offered.

A short distance in his front was the village of Podelwitz. Behind his position were two elevations, on which he placed his guns, forty in number. In rear of these elevations was a very thick wood. The Imperialist right was commanded by Fürstenberg, the left by Pappenheim, the center by Tilly himself. Although he had yielded to his generals so far as to take up a position on the plain, Tilly was resolved, if possible, not to fight until the arrival of the reinforcements; but the rashness of Pappenheim brought on a battle. To approach the Austrian position the Swedes had to cross the little river

Loder, and Pappenheim asked permission of Tilly to charge them as they did so. Tilly consented on condition that he only charged with two thousand horse and did not bring on a general engagement. Accordingly, as the Scottish brigade under Sir James Ramsay crossed the Loder, Pappenheim swept down upon them.

The Scots stood firm, and with pike and musket repelled the attack; and after hard fighting Pappenheim was obliged to fall back, setting fire as he retired to the village of Podelwitz. The smoke of the burning village drifted across the plain, and was useful to the Swedes, as under its cover the entire army passed the Loder, and formed up ready for battle facing the Imperialists' position, the movement being executed under a heavy fire from the Austrian batteries on the hills.

The Swedish order of battle was different from that of the Imperialists. The latter had their cavalry massed together in one heavy, compact body, while the Swedish regiments of horse were placed alternately with the various regiments or brigades of infantry. The Swedish center was composed of four brigades of pikemen. Guns were behind the first line, as were the cavalry supporting the pikemen. The regiments of musketeers were placed at intervals among the brigades of pikemen.

Pappenheim on his return to the camp ordered up the whole of his cavalry, and charged down with fury upon the Swedes, while at the same moment Furstenberg dashed with seven regiments of cavalry on the Saxons. Between these and the Swedes there was a slight interval, for Gustavus had doubts of the steadiness of his allies, and was anxious that in case of their defeat his own troops should not be thrown into confusion. The result justified his anticipations.

Attacked with fury on their flank by Fürstenberg's horse, while his infantry and artillery poured a direct fire into their front, the Saxons at once gave way. Their elector was the first to set the example of flight and, turning his horse, galloped without drawing rein to Torgau, and in twenty minutes after the commencement of the fight the whole of the Saxons were in utter rout, hotly pursued by Fürstenberg's cavalry.

Tilly now deemed the victory certain, for nearly half of his opponents were disposed of, and he outnumbered the remainder by two to one; but while Fürstenberg had gained so complete a victory over the Saxons, Pappenheim, who had charged the Swedish center, had met with a very different reception.

In vain he tried to break through the Swedish spears. The wind was blowing full in the faces of the pikemen, and the clouds of smoke and dust which rolled down upon them rendered it impossible for them to see the heavy columns of horse until they fell upon them like an avalanche, yet with perfect steadiness they withstood the attacks.

Seven times Pappenheim renewed his charge; seven times he fell back broken and disordered.

As he drew off for the last time Gustavus, seeing the rout of the Saxons, and knowing that he would have the whole of Tilly's force upon him in a few minutes, determined to rid himself altogether of Pappenheim and launched the whole of his cavalry upon the retreating squadrons with overwhelming effect. Thus at the end of half an hour's fighting Tilly had disposed of the Saxons and Gustavus had driven Pappenheim's horse from the field.

Three of the Scottish regiments were sent from the center to strengthen Horn on the left flank, which was now exposed by the flight of the Saxons. Scarcely had the Scottish musketeers taken their position when Furstenberg's horse returned triumphant from their pursuit of the Saxons and at once fell upon Horn's pikemen. These, however, stood as firmly as their comrades in the center had done; and the Scottish musketeers, six deep, the three front ranks kneeling, the three in rear standing, poured such heavy volleys into the horsemen that these fell back in disorder; the more confused perhaps, since volley firing was at that time peculiar to the Swedish army, and the crashes of musketry were new to the Imperialists.

As the cavalry fell back in disorder, Gustavus led his horse, who had just returned from the pursuit of Pappenheim, against them. The shock was irresistible, and Furstenberg's horse were driven headlong from the field. But the Imperialist infantry, led by Tilly himself, were now close at hand, and the roar of musketry along the whole line was tremendous, while the artillery on both sides played unceasingly.

Just as the battle was at the hottest the Swedish reserve came up to the assistance of the first line, and Sir John Hepburn led the Green Brigade through the intervals of the Swedish regiments into action. Lord Reay's regiment was in front and Munro, leading it on, advanced against the solid Imperialist columns, pouring heavy volleys into them. When close at hand the pikemen passed through the intervals of the musketeers and charged furiously with leveled pikes, the musketeers following them with clubbed weapons.

The gaps formed by the losses of the regiment at New Brandenburg and the other engagements had been filled up, and two thousand strong they fell upon the Imperialists. For a few minutes there was a tremendous hand-to-hand conflict, but the valor and strength of the Scotch prevailed, and the regiment was the first to burst its way through the ranks of the Imperialists, and then pressed on to attack the trenches behind, held by the Walloon infantry.

While the battle was raging in the plain the Swedish cavalry, after driving away Fürstenberg's horse, swept round and charged the eminence in the rear of the Imperialists, cutting down the artillerymen and capturing the cannon there.

These were at once turned upon the masses of Imperialists infantry, who thus, taken between two fires—pressed hotly by the pikemen in front, mown down by the cannon in their rear—lost heart and fled precipitately, four regiments alone, the veterans of Fürstenberg's infantry, holding together and cutting their way through to the woods in the rear of their position.

The slaughter would have been even greater than it was, had not the cloud of dust and smoke been so thick that the Swedes were unable to see ten yards in front of them. The pursuit was taken up by their cavalry, who pressed the flying Imperialists until nightfall. So complete was the defeat that Tilly, who was badly wounded, could only muster six hundred men to accompany him in his retreat, and Pappenheim could get together but fourteen hundred of his horsemen. Seven thousand of the Imperialists were killed, five thousand were wounded or taken prisoners. The Swedes lost but seven hundred men, the Saxons about two thousand.

The Swedes that night occupied the Imperial tents, making great bonfires of the broken wagons, pikes, and stockades. A hundred standards were taken. Tilly had fought throughout the battle with desperate valor. He was ever in the van of his infantry and three times was wounded by bullets and once taken prisoner, and only rescued after a desperate conflict.

At the conclusion of the day Cronenberg with six hundred Walloon cavalry threw themselves around him and bore him from the field. The fierce old soldier is said to have burst into a passion of tears on beholding the slaughter and defeat of his infantry. Hitherto he had been invincible, this being the first defeat he had suffered in the course of his long military career. Great stores of provision had been captured, and the night was spent in feasting in the Swedish camp.

The next morning the elector of Saxony rode on to the field to congratulate Gustavus on his victory. The latter was politic enough to receive him with great courtesy and to thank him for the services the Saxons had rendered. He intrusted to the elector the task of recapturing Leipzig, while he marched against Merseburg, which he captured with its garrison of five hundred men.

After two or three assaults had been made on Leipzig the garrison capitulated to the Saxons, and on the 11th of September the army was drawn up and reviewed by Gustavus. When the king arrived opposite the Green Brigade he dismounted and made the soldiers an address, thanking them for their great share in winning the battle of Leipzig.

Many of the Scottish officers were promoted, Munro being made a full colonel, and many others advanced a step in rank. The Scottish brigade responded heartily to the address of the gallant king with hearty cheers. Gustavus was indeed beloved as well as admired by his soldiers. Fearless himself of danger, he ever recognized bravery in others, and was ready to take his full share of every hardship as well as every peril.

He had ever a word of commendation and encouragement for his troops, and was regarded by them as a comrade as well as a leader. In person he was tall and rather stout, his face was handsome, his complexion fair, his forehead lofty, his hair auburn, his eyes large and penetrating, his cheeks ruddy and healthy. He had an air of majesty which enabled him to address his soldiers in terms of cheerful familiarity without in the slightest degree dimishing their respect and reverence for him as their monarch.

CHAPTER X.

THE PASSAGE OF THE RHINE.

"I suppose," Nigel Græme said, as the officers of the regiment assembled in one of the Imperialist tents on the night after the battle of Leipzig, "we shall at once press forward to Vienna;" and such was the general opinion throughout the Swedish army; but such was not the intention of Gustavus. Undoubtedly the temptation to press forward and dictate peace in Vienna was strong, but the difficulties and disadvantages of such a step were many. He had but twenty thousand men, for the Saxons could not be reckoned upon; and indeed it was probable that their elector, whose jealousy and dislike of Gustavus would undoubtedly be heightened by the events of the battle of Breitenfeld, would prove himself to be a more than doubtful ally were the Swedish army to remove to a distance.

Tilly would soon rally his fugitives and, reinforced by the numerous Imperialist garrisons from the towns, would be able to overrun North Germany in his absence and to force the Saxons to join him even if the elector were unwilling to do so. Thus the little Swedish force would be isolated in the heart of Germany; and should Ferdinand abandon Vienna at his approach and altogether refuse to treat with him—which his obstinacy upon a former occasion, when in the very hands of his enemy, rendered probable—the Swedes would find themselves in a desperate position, isolated and alone in the midst of enemies.

There was another consideration. An Imperialist diet was at that moment sitting at Frankfort, and Ferdinand was using all his influence to compel the various princes and representatives of the free cities to submit to him. It was of the utmost importance that Gustavus should strengthen his friends and overawe the waverers by the approach of his army. Hitherto Franconia and the Rhine provinces had been entirely in the hands of the Imperialists, and it was needful that a counterbalancing influence should be exerted. These considerations induced Gustavus to abandon the tempting idea of a march upon Vienna. The elector of Saxony was charged with carrying the war into Silesia and Bohemia, the electors of Hesse and Hesse-Cassel were to maintain Lower Saxony and Westphalia, and the Swedish army turned its face toward the Rhine.

On the 20th of September it arrived before Erfurt, an important fortified town on the Gera, which surrendered at discretion. Gustavus granted the inhabitants, who were for the most part Catholics, the free exercise of their religion, and nominated the Duke of Saxe-Weimar to be governor of the district and of the province of Thüringen, and the Count of

Löwenstein to be commander of the garrison, which consisted of Colonel Foulis' Scottish regiment, one thousand five hundred strong.

Traveling by different routes in two columns the army marched to Würtzburg, the capital of Franconia, a rich and populous city, the Imperialist garrison having withdrawn to the strong castle of Marienburg, on a lofty eminence overlooking the town, and only separated from it by the river Main. The cathedral at Würtzburg is dedicated to a Scottish saint, St. Kilian, a bishop who, with two priests came from Scotland in the year 688 to convert the heathens of Franconia. They baptized many at Würtzburg, among them Gospert, the duke of that country. This leader was married to Geilana, the widow of his brother; and Kilian urging upon him that such a marriage was contrary to the laws of the Christian church, the duke promised to separate from her. Geilana had not, like her lord, accepted Christianity and, furious at this interference of Kilian, she seized the opportunity when the latter had gone with his followers on an expedition against the pagan Saxons to have Kilian and his two companions murdered.

The cathedral was naturally an object of interest to the Scotch soldiers in the time of Gustavus, and there was an animated argument in the quarters of the officers of Munro's regiment on the night of their arrival as to whether St. Kilian had done well or otherwise in insisting upon his new convert repudiating his wife. The general opinion, however, was against the saint, the colonel summing up the question.

"In my opinion," he said, "Kilian was a fool. Here was no less a matter at stake than the conversion of a whole nation, or at least of a great tribe of heathens, and Kilian imperiled it all on a question of minor importance; for in the first place, the Church of Rome has always held that the pope could grant permission for marriage within interdicted degrees; in the second place, the marriage had taken place before the conversion of the duke to Christianity, and they were therefore innocently and without thought of harm *bona fide* man and wife. Lastly, the Church of Rome is opposed to divorce; and Kilian might in any case have put up with this small sin, if sin it were, for the sake of saving the souls of thousands of pagans. My opinion is that St. Kilian richly deserved the fate which befell him. And now to a subject much more interesting to us—viz. the capture of Marienburg.

"I tell you, my friends, it is going to be a warm business; the castle is considered impregnable, and is strong by nature as well as art, and Captain Keller is said to be a stout and brave soldier. He has one thousand men in the garrison, and all the monks who were in the town have gone up and turned soldiers. But if the task is a hard one the reward will be rich; for as the Imperialists believe the place cannot be taken, the treasures of all the country round are stored up there. And I can tell you more. In the cellars are sixty gigantic tuns of stone, the smallest of which holds twenty-five wagon loads of provisions, and they say it is all of the highest quality. With glory and treasure and good food to be won we will out-do ourselves to-morrow; and you may be sure that the brunt of the affair will fall upon the Scots."

"Well, there is one satisfaction," said Nigel Graeme—who after Leipzig had been promoted to the rank of major—"if we get the lion's share of the fighting, we shall have the lion's share of the plunder."

"For shame, Graeme! You say nothing of the glory."

"Ah, well," Graeme laughed, "we have already had so large a share of that, that I for one could do without winning any more just at present. It's a dear commodity to purchase, and neither fills our belly nor our pockets."

"For shame, Graeme! for shame!" Munro said laughing. "It is a shame that such sentiments should be whispered in the Scottish brigade; and now to bed, gentlemen, for we shall have, methinks, a busy day to-morrow."

Sir James Ramsay was appointed to command the assault. The river Main had to be crossed, and he sent off Lieutenant Robert Ramsay of his own regiment to obtain boats from the peasantry. The disguise in which he went was seen through, and he was taken prisoner and carried to the castle. A few boats were, however, obtained by the Swedes. The river is here three hundred yards wide, and the central arch of the bridge had been blown up by the Imperialists, a single plank remaining across the chasm over the river forty-eight feet below. The bridge was swept by the heaviest cannon in the fortress, and a passage appeared well-nigh hopeless. On the afternoon of the 5th of October the party prepared to pass, some in boats, others by the bridge. A tremendous fire was opened by the Imperialists from cannon and musketry, sweeping the bridge with a storm of missiles and lashing the river to foam around the boats. The soldiers in these returned the fire with their muskets, and the smoke served as a cover to conceal them from the enemy.

In the meantime Major Bothwell of Ramsay's regiment led a company across the bridge. These, in spite of the fire, crossed the plank over the broken arch and reached the head of the bridge, from whence they kept up so heavy a fire upon the gunners and musketeers in the lower works by the river that they forced them to quit their posts, and so enabled Sir James Ramsay and Sir John Hamilton to effect a landing. Major Bothwell, his brother, and the greater part of his followers were, however, slain by the Imperialists' fire from above. The commandant of the castle now sallied out and endeavored to recapture the works by the water, but the Scotch repelled the attack and drove the enemy up the hill to the castle again. The Scottish troops having thus effected a lodgment across the river, and being protected by the rocks from the enemy's fire, lay down for the night in the position they had won.

Gustavus during the night caused planks to be thrown across the broken bridge and prepared to assault at daybreak. Just as morning was breaking, a Swedish officer with seven men climbed up the hill to reconnoitre the castle, and found to his surprise that the drawbridge was down, but a guard of two hundred men were stationed at the gate.

He was at once challenged and, shouting "Sweden!" sprang with his men on to the end of the drawbridge. The Imperialists tried in vain to raise it; before they could succeed some companions of the Swedes ran up and, driving in the guard, took possession of the outer court.

Almost at the same moment Ramsay's and Hamilton's regiments commenced their assault on a strong outwork of the castle, which, after two hours' desperate fighting, they succeeded in gaining. They then turned its guns upon the gate of the keep, which they battered down and were about to charge in when they received orders from the king to halt and retire, while the Swedish regiment of Axel-Lilly and the Blue Brigade advanced to the storm.

The Scottish regiments retired in the deepest discontent, deeming themselves affronted by others being ordered to the post of honor after they had by their bravery cleared the way. The Swedish troops forced their way in after hard fighting; and the Castle of Marienburg, so long deemed impregnable, was captured after a few hours' fighting. The quantity of treasure found in it was enormous, and there were sufficient provisions to have lasted its garrison for twenty years.

Immediately the place was taken Colonel Sir John Hamilton advanced to Gustavus and resigned his commission on the spot; nor did the assurances of the king that he intended no insult to the Scotch soldiers mollify his wrath, and quitting the Swedish service he returned at once to Scotland. Munro's regiment had taken no part in the storming of Marienburg, but was formed up on the north side of the river in readiness to advance should the first attack be repelled, and many were wounded by the shot of the enemy while thus inactive.

Malcolm while binding up the arm of his sergeant who stood next to him felt a sharp pain shoot through his leg, and at once fell to the ground. He was lifted up and carried to the rear, where his wound was examined by the doctor to the regiment.

"Your luck has not deserted you," he said after probing the wound. "The bullet had missed the bone by half an inch and a short rest will soon put you right again."

Fortunately for a short time the army remained around Würtzburg. Columns scoured the surrounding country, capturing the various towns and fortresses held by the Imperialists, and collecting large quantities of provisions and stores. Tilly's army lay within a few days' march; but although superior in numbers to that of Gustavus, Tilly had received strict orders not to risk a general engagement as his army was now almost the only one that remained to the Imperialists, and should it suffer another defeat the country would lie at the mercy of the Swedes.

One evening when Malcolm had so far recovered as to be able to walk for a short distance, he was at supper with Colonel Munro and some other officers, when the door opened and Gustavus himself entered. All leaped to their feet.

"Munro," he said, "get the musketeers of your brigade under arms with all haste, form them up in the square before the townhall, and desire Sir John Hepburn to meet me there."

The drums were at once beaten, and the troops came pouring from their lodgings, and in three or four minutes the musketeers, eight hundred strong, were formed up with Hepburn and Munro at their head. Malcolm had prepared to take his arms on the summons, but Munro said at once:

"No, Malcolm, so sudden a summons augurs desperate duty, maybe a long night march; you would break down before you got half a mile; besides, as only the musketeers have to go, half the officers must remain here."

Without a word the king placed himself at the head of the men, and through the dark and stormy night the troops started on their unknown mission. Hepburn and Munro were, like their men, on foot, for they had not had time to have their horses saddled.

After marching two hours along the right bank

of the Main the tramp of horses was heard behind them, and they were reinforced by eighty troopers whom Gustavus before starting had ordered to mount and follow. Hitherto the king had remained lost in abstraction, but he now roused himself.

"I have just received the most serious news, Hepburn. Tilly has been reinforced by seventeen thousand men under the duke of Lorraine, and is marching with all speed against me. Were my whole army collected here he would outnumber us by two to one, but many columns are away, and the position is well-nigh desperate.

"I have resolved to hold Ochsenfurt. The place is not strong, but it lies in a sharp bend of the river and may be defended for a time. If any can do so it is surely you and your Scots. Tilly is already close to the town; indeed the man who brought me the news said that when he left it his advanced pickets were just entering, hence the need for this haste.

"You must hold it to the last, Hepburn, and then, if you can, fall back to Würtzburg; even a day's delay will enable me to call in some of the detachments and to prepare to receive Tilly."

Without halting, the little column marched sixteen miles, and then, crossing the bridge over the Main, entered Ochsenfurt.

It was occupied by a party of fifty Imperialist arquebusiers, but these were driven headlong from it. The night was extremely dark, all were ignorant of the locality, and the troops were formed up in the market-place to await either morning or the attack of Tilly. Fifty troopers were sent half a mile in advance to give warning of the approach of the enemy. They had scarcely taken their place when they were attacked by the Imperialists, who had been roused by the firing in the town. The incessant flash of fire and the heavy rattle of musketry told Gustavus that they were in force, and a lieutenant of Lumsden's regiment with fifty musketeers was sent off to reinforce the cavalry. The Imperialists were, however, too strong to be checked, and horse and foot were being driven in when Colonel Munro sallied out with a hundred of his own regiment, and the Imperialists after a brisk skirmish, not knowing what force they had to deal with, fell back.

As soon as day broke the king and Hepburn made a tour of the walls, which were found to be in a very bad condition and ill-calculated to resist an assault. The Imperialists were not to be seen, and the king, fearing they might have marched by some other route against Würtzburg, determined to return at once, telling Hepburn to mind the bridge, and to blow it up if forced to abandon the town.

Hepburn at once set to work to strengthen the position, to demolish all the houses and walls outside the defenses, cut down and destroy all trees and hedges which might shelter an enemy, and to strengthen the walls with banks of earth and platforms of wood. For three days the troops labored incessantly; on the third night the enemy were heard approaching. The advanced troopers and a half company of infantry were driven in, contesting every foot of the way. When they reached the walls heavy volleys were poured in by the musketeers who lined them upon the approaching enemy, and Tilly, supposing that Gustavus must have moved forward a considerable portion of his army, called off his troops and marched away to Nuremberg. Two days later Hepburn was ordered to return with his force to Würtzburg.

The king now broke up his camp near Würtzburg, and leaving a garrison in the castle of Marienburg and appointing Marshal Horn to hold Franconia with eight thousand men, he marched against Frankfort-on-the-Main, his troops capturing all the towns and castles on the way, levying contributions, and collecting great booty. Frankfort opened its gates without resistance, and for a short time the army had rest in pleasant quarters.

The regiments were reorganized, in some cases two of those which had suffered most being joined into one. Gustavus had lately been strengthened by two more Scottish regiments under Sir Frederick Hamilton and Alexander, Master of Forbes, and an English regiment under Captain Austin. He had now thirteen regiments of Scottish infantry, and the other corps of the army were almost entirely officered by Scotchmen. He had five regiments of English and Irish, and had thus eighteen regiments of British infantry.

At Frankfort he was joined by the marquis of Hamilton, who had done splendid service with the troops under his command. He had driven the Imperialists out of Silesia, and marching south, struck such fear into them that Tilly was obliged to weaken his army to send reinforcements to that quarter. By the order of Gustavus he left Silesia and marched to Magdeburg. He had now but three thousand five hundred men with him, two thousand seven hundred having died from pestilence, famine and disease. He assisted General Banner in blockading the Imperialist garrison of Magdeburg, and his losses by fever and pestilence thinned his troops down to two small regiments; these were incorporated with the force of the duke of Saxe-Weimar, and the marquis of Hamilton joined the staff of Gustavus as a simple volunteer.

The king now determined to conquer the Palatinate, which was held by a Spanish army. He drove them before him until he reached the Rhine, where they endeavored to defend the passage by burning every vessel and boat they could find, and for a time the advance of the Swedes was checked. It was now the end of November, the snow lay thick over the whole country, and the troops, without tents or covering, were bivouacked along the side of the river, two miles below Oppenheim. The opposite bank was covered with bushes to the water's edge, and on an eminence a short distance back could be seen the tents of the Spaniards.

"If it were summer we might swim across," Nigel

Græme said to Malcolm; "the river is broad, but a good swimmer could cross it easily enough."

"Yes," Malcolm agreed, "there would be no difficulty in swimming if unencumbered with arms and armor, but there would be no advantage in getting across without these; if we could but get hold of a boat or two, we would soon wake yonder Spaniards up."

The next morning Malcolm wandered along the bank closely examining the bushes as he went, to see if any boats might be concealed among them, for the fishermen and boatmen would naturally try to save their craft when they heard that the Imperialists were destroying them. He walked three miles up the river without success. As he returned he kept his eyes fixed on the bushes on the opposite bank. When within half a mile of the camp he suddenly stopped, for his eye caught something dark among them. He went to the water's edge and stooped, the better to see under the bushes, and saw what he doubted not to be the stern of a boat hauled up and sheltered beneath them. He leaped to his feet with a joyful exclamation. Here was the means of crossing the river; but the boat had to be brought over.

Once afloat this would be easy enough, but he was sure that his own strength would be insufficient to launch her, and that he should need the aid of at least one man. On returning to camp he called aside the sergeant of his company, James Grant, who was from his own estate in Nithsdale, and whom he knew to be a good swimmer.

"Sergeant," he said, "I want you to join me in an enterprise to-night. I have found a boat hauled up under the bushes on the opposite shore, and we must bring her across. I cannot make out her size; but from the look of her stern I should say she was a large boat. You had better therefore borrow from the artillerymen one of their wooden levers, and get a stout pole two or three inches across, and cut half a dozen two-foot lengths from it to put under her as rollers. Get also a plank of four inches wide from one of the deserted houses in the village behind us, and cut out two paddles; we may find oars on board, but it is as well to be prepared in case the owner should have removed them."

"Shall I take my weapons, sir?"

"We can take our dirks in our belts, sergeant, and lash our swords to the wooden lever, but I do not think we shall have any fighting. The night will be dark, and the Spaniards, believing that we have no boats, will not keep a very strict watch. The worst part of the business is the swim across the river, the water will be bitterly cold; but as you and I have often swum Scotch burns when they were swollen by the melting snow I think that we may well manage to get across this sluggish stream."

"At what time will we be starting, sir?"

"Be here at the edge of the river at six o'clock, sergeant. I can get away at that time without exciting comment, and we will say nothing about it unless we succeed."

Thinking it over, however, it occurred to Malcolm that by this means a day would be lost, and he knew how anxious the king was to press forward. He therefore abandoned his idea of keeping his discovery secret, and going to his colonel reported that he had found a boat and could bring it across from the other side by seven o'clock.

The news was so important that Munro at once went to the king. Gustavus ordered three hundred Swedes and a hundred Scots of each of the regiments of Ramsay, Munro, and the laird of Wormiston, the whole under the command of Count Brahé, to form up after dark on the river bank and prepare to cross, and he himself came down to superintend the passage. By six it was perfectly dark. During the day Malcolm had placed two stones on the edge of the water, one exactly opposite the boat, the other twenty feet behind it in an exact line. When Gustavus arrived at the spot where the troops were drawn up, Malcolm was taken up to him by his colonel.

"Well, my brave young Græme," the king said, "so you are going to do us another service; but how will you find the boat in this darkness? Even were there no stream you would find it very difficult to strike the exact spot on a dark night like this."

"I have provided against that, sir, by placing two marks on the bank. When we start, lanterns will be placed on these. We shall cross higher up so as to strike the bank a little above where I believe the boat to be, then we shall float along under the bushes until the lanterns are in a line one with another, and we shall know then that we are exactly opposite the boat."

"Well thought of!" the king exclaimed. "Munro, this lieutenant of yours is a treasure. And now God speed you, my friend, in your cold swim across the stream!"

Malcolm and the sergeant now walked half a mile up the river, a distance which, judging from the strength of the current and the speed at which they could swim, would, they thought, take them to the opposite bank at about the point where the boat was lying. Shaking hands with Colonel Munro, who had accompanied them, Malcolm entered the icy-cold water without delay. Knowing that it was possible that their strength might give out before they reached the opposite side, Malcolm had had two pairs of small casks lashed two feet apart. These they fastened securely, so that as they began to swim the casks floated a short distance behind each shoulder, giving them perfect support. The lever and paddles were towed behind them. The lights in the two camps afforded them a means of directing their way. The water was intensely cold, and before they were half-way across Malcolm congratulated himself upon having thought of the casks. Had it not been for them he would have began to doubt his ability to reach the further shore, for although he would have thought nothing of the swim at other times his limbs were fast becoming numbed with the extreme cold. The sergeant kept close to him, and a word or two was occasionally exchanged.

"I think it is colder than our mountain streams, Grant."

"It's no colder, your honor, but the water is smooth and still, and we do not have to wrestle with it as with a brook in spate. It's the stillness which makes it feel so cold. The harder we swim the less we will feel it."

It was with a deep feeling of relief that Malcolm saw something loom just in front of him from the darkness, and knew that he was close to the land. A few more strokes and he touched the bushes. Looking back he saw that the two lights were nearly in a line. Stopping swimming he let the stream drift him down. Two or three minutes more and one of the tiny lights seemed exactly above the other.

"This is the spot, Grant," he said in a low voice; "land here as quietly as you can."

CHAPTER XI.

THE CAPTURE OF OPPENHEIM.

The two swimmers dragged themselves on shore, but for a minute or two could scarce stand, so numbed were their limbs by the cold. Malcolm took from his belt a flask of brandy, took a long draught, and handed it to his companion who followed his example.

The spirit sent a glow of warmth through their veins, and they began to search among the bushes for the boat, one proceeding each way along the bank. They had not removed their leathern doublets before entering the water, as these, buoyed up as they were, would not affect their swimming, and would be a necessary protection when they landed not only against the cold of the night air but against the bushes.

Malcolm's beacon proved an accurate guide, for he had not proceeded twenty yards before he came against a solid object which he at once felt to be the boat. A low whistle called the sergeant to his side, bringing with him the rollers and paddles from the spot where they had landed. They soon felt that the boat was a large one, and that their strength would have been wholly insufficient to get her into the water without the aid of the lever and rollers. Taking the former they placed its end under the stern-post, and placing a roller under its heel to serve as a pivot they threw their weight on the other end of the lever and at once raised the boat some inches in the air.

Grant held the lever down and Malcolm slid a roller as far up under the keel as it would go; the lever was then shifted and the boat again raised, and the process was continued until her weight rested upon three rollers. She was now ready to be launched, and as the bank was steep they had no doubt of their ability to run her down. An examination had already shown that their paddles would be needless, as the oars were inside her. They took their places one on each side of the bow, and applying their strength the boat glided rapidly down.

"Gently, Grant," Malcolm said, "don't let her go in with a splash. There may be some sentries within hearing." They continued their work cautiously, and the boat noiselessly entered the water. Getting out the oars they gave her a push, and she was soon floating down the stream. The rowlocks were in their places, and rowing with extreme care so as to avoid making the slightest sound they made their way across the river. They were below the camp when they landed, but there were many men on the lookout, for the news of the attempt had spread rapidly.

Leaping ashore amidst a low cheer from a group of soldiers, Malcolm directed them to tow the boat up at once to the place where the troops were formed ready for crossing, while he and the sergeant, who were both chilled to the bone, for their clothes had frozen stiff upon them, hurried to the spot where the regiment was bivouacked. Here by the side of a blazing fire they stripped, and were rubbed with cloths by their comrades till a glow of warmth again began to be felt, the external heat and friction being aided by the administration of steaming cups of hot tea. Dry clothes were taken from their knapsacks and warmed before the fire, and when these were put on they again felt warm and comfortable.

Hurrying off now to the spot where the troops were drawn up, they found the boat had already made two passages. She rowed four oars, and would, laden down to the water's edge, carry twenty-five men. The oars had been muffled with cloths so as to make no sound in the rowlocks. A party of Munro's Scots had first crossed, then a party of Swedes. Malcolm and the sergeant joined their company unnoticed in the darkness. Each detachment sent over a boat load in turns, and when six loads had crossed it was again the turn of the men in Munro's regiment, and Malcolm entered the boat with the men. The lights still burned as a signal, enabling the boat to land each party almost at the same spot. Malcolm wondered what was going on. A perfect stillness reigned on the other side, and it was certain that the alarm had not yet been given.

On ascending the bank he saw in front of him some dark figures actively engaged, and heard dull sounds. On reaching the spot he found the parties who had preceded him hard at work with shovels throwing up an intrenchment. In the darkness he had not perceived that each of the soldiers carried a spade in addition to his arms. The soil was deep and soft, and the operations were carried on with scarce a sound. As each party landed they fell to work under the direction of their officers. All night the labor continued, and when the dull light of the winter morning began to dispel the darkness a solid rampart of earth breast-high rose in a semicircle, with its two extremities resting on the riverbank.

The last boat load had but just arrived across, and the six hundred men were now gathered in the work, which was about one hundred and fifty feet across, the base formed by the river. The earth forming the ramparts had been taken from the outside, and a ditch three feet deep and six feet wide had been thus formed.

The men who, in spite of the cold, were hot and perspiring from their night's work, now entered the intrenched space and sat down to take a meal, each man having brought two days' rations in his haversack. It grew rapidly lighter, and suddenly the sound of a trumpet, followed by the rapid beating of drums, showed that the Spaniards had, from their camp on the eminence half a mile away, discovered the work which had sprung up during the night as if by magic on their side of the river.

In a few minutes a great body of cavalry was seen issuing from the Spanish camp, and fourteen squadrons of cuirassiers trotted down toward the intrenchments. Soon the word was given to charge, and, like a torrent, the mass of cavalry swept down upon it.

Two-thirds of those who had crossed were musketeers, the remainder pikemen. The latter formed the front line behind the rampart, their spears forming a close hedge around it, while the musketeers prepared to fire between them. By the order of Count Brahé not a trigger was pulled until the cavalry were within fifty yards, then a flash of flame swept round the rampart, and horses and men in the front line of the cavalry tumbled to the ground. But half the musketeers had fired, and a few seconds later another volley was poured into the horsemen. The latter, however, although many had fallen, did not check their speed, but rose up close to the rampart, and flung themselves upon the hedge of spears.

Nothing could exceed the gallantry with which the Spaniards fought. Some dismounted and, leaping into the ditch, tried to climb the rampart; others leaped the horses into it, and standing up in their saddles, cut at the spearmen with their swords and fired their pistols among them. Many, again, tried to leap their horses over ditch and rampart, but the pikemen stood firm, while at short intervals withering volleys tore into the struggling mass.

For half an hour the desperate fight continued, and then, finding that the position could not be carried by horsemen, the Spanish commander drew off his men, leaving no less than six hundred lying dead around the rampart of earth. There were no Spanish infantry within some miles of the spot, and the cavalry rode away, some to Maintz, but the greater part to Oppenheim, where there was a strong garrison of one thousand men.

A careful search among the bushes brought three more boats to light, and a force was soon taken across the river sufficient to maintain itself against any attack. Gustavus himself was in one of the first boats that crossed.

"Well done, my brave hearts!" he said as he landed, just as the Spanish horsemen had ridden away. "You have fought stoutly and well, and our way is now open to us. Where are Lieutenant Græme and the sergeant who swam across with him?"

Malcolm and his companion soon presented themselves.

"I sent for you to your camp," the king said, "but found that you but waited to change your clothes, and had then joined the force crossing. You had no orders to do so."

"We had no orders not to do so, sire, but having begun the affair it was only natural that we should see the end of it."

"You had done your share and more," the king said, "and I thank you both heartily for it, and promote you, Græme, at once to the rank of captain, and will request Colonel Munro to give you the first company which may fall vacant in his regiment. If a vacancy should not occur shortly I will place you in another regiment until one may happen in your own corps. To you, sergeant, I give a commission as officer. You will take that rank at once, and will be a supernumerary in your regiment till a vacancy occurs. Such promotion has been well and worthily won by you both."

Without delay an advance was ordered against Oppenheim. It lay on the Imperialist side of the Rhine. Behind the town stood a strong and well-fortified castle upon a lofty eminence. Its guns swept not only the country around it, but the ground upon the opposite side of the river. There, facing it, stood a strong fort surrounded by double ditches, which were deep and broad and full of water. They were crossed only by a drawbridge on the side facing the river, and the garrison could therefore obtain by boats supplies or reinforcements as needed from the town.

The Green and Blue Brigades at once commenced opening trenches against this fort, and would have assaulted the place without delay had not a number of boats been brought over by a Protestant well-wisher of the Swedes from the other side of the river. The assault was therefore delayed in order that the attack might be delivered simultaneously against the positions on both sides of the river. The brigade of guards and the White Brigade crossed in the boats at Gernsheim, five miles from the town, and marched against it during the night.

The Spaniards from their lofty position in the castle of Oppenheim saw the camp-fires of the Scots around their fort on the other side of the river and opened a heavy cannonade upon them. The fire was destructive and many of the Scots were killed, Hepburn and Munro having a narrow escape, a cannon ball passing just over their heads as they were sitting together by a fire.

The defenders of the fort determined to take advantage of the fire poured upon their assailants, and two hundred musketeers made a gallant sortie upon them; but Hepburn led on his pikemen who were nearest at hand, and, without firing a shot, drove them back again into the fort. At daybreak the roar of cannon on the opposite side of the river commenced, and showed that the king with the divisions which had crossed had arrived at their posts. The governor of the fort, seeing that, if, as was certain, the lower town were captured by the Swedes, he should be cut off from all communication with the castle and completely isolated, surrendered to Sir John Hepburn.

The town had, indeed, at once opened its gates, and two hundred men of Sir James Ramsay's regiment were placed there. Hepburn prepared to cross the river with the Blue and Green Brigades to aid the king in reducing the castle—a place of vast size and strength—whose garrison, composed of Spaniards and Italians, were replying to the fire of Gustavus. A boat was lying at the gate of the fort.

"Captain Græme," Hepburn said to Malcolm,

"take with you two lieutenants and twenty men in the boat and cross the river; then send word by an officer to the king that the fort here has surrendered, and that I am about to cross, and let the men bring over that flotilla of boats which is lying under the town wall."

Malcolm crossed at once. After dispatching the message to the king and sending the officer back with the boats he had for the moment nothing to do, and made his way into the town to inquire from the officers of Ramsay's detachment how things were going. He found the men drawn up.

"Ah! Malcolm Græme," the major in command said, "you have arrived in the very nick of time to take part in a gallant enterprise."

"I am ready," Malcolm said; "what is to be done?"

"We are going to take the castle, that is all," the major said.

"You are joking," Malcolm laughed, looking at the great castle and the little band of two hundred men.

"That am I not," the major answered, "my men have just discovered a private passage from the governor's quarters here up to the very gate of the outer wall. As you see we have collected some ladders, and as we shall take them by surprise, while they are occupied with the king, we shall give a good account of them."

"I will go with you right willingly," Malcolm said; but he could not but feel that the enterprise was a desperate one, and wished that the major had waited until a few hundred more men had crossed. Placing himself behind the Scottish officer, he advanced up the passage which had been discovered. Ascending flight after flight of stone stairs, the column issued from the passage at the very foot of the outer wall before the garrison stationed there were aware of their approach. The ladders were just placed when the Italians caught sight of them and rushed to the defense, but it was too late. The Scotch swarmed up and gained a footing on the wall.

Driving the enemy before them they cleared the outer works and pressed so hotly upon the retiring Imperialists that they entered with them into the inner works of the castle, crossing the drawbridge over the moat which separated it from its outer works before the garrison had time to raise it.

Now in the very heart of the castle a terrible encounter took place. The garrison, twelve hundred strong, ran down from their places on the wall, and seeing how small was the force that had entered fell upon them with fury. It was a hand to hand fight. Loud rose the war-cries of the Italian and Spanish soldiers, and the answering cheers of the Scots mingled with the clash of sword on steel armor and the cries of the wounded, while without the walls the cannon of Gustavus thundered incessantly.

Not since the dreadful struggle in the streets of New Brandenburg had Malcolm been engaged in so desperate a strife. All order and regularity was lost, and man to man they fought with pike, sword and clubbed musket. There was no giving of orders, for no word could be heard in such a din, and the officers with their swords and halfpikes fought desperately in the melée with the rest. Gradually, however, the strength and endurance of Ramsay's veterans prevailed over numbers. Most of the officers of the Imperialists had been slain as well as their bravest men, and the rest began to draw off and to scatter through the castle, some to look for hiding places, many to jump over the walls rather than fall into the hands of the terrible Scots.

The astonishment of Gustavus and of Hepburn, who was now marching with his men toward the castle, at hearing the rattle of musketry and the din of battle within the very heart of the fortress was great indeed, and this was heightened when, a few minutes later, the soldiers were seen leaping desperately from the walls, and a great shout arose from the troops as the Imperial banner was seen to descend from its flagstaff on the keep. Gustavus with his staff rode at once to the gate which was opened for him, and on entering he found Ramsay's little force drawn up to salute him as he entered. It was reduced nearly half in strength, and not a man but was bleeding from several wounds, while cleft helms and dinted armor showed how severe had been the fray.

"My brave Scots," he exclaimed, "why were you too quick for me?"

The courtyard of the castle was piled with slain,

who were also scattered in every room throughout it, five hundred having been slain there before the rest threw down their arms and were given quarter. This exploit was one of the most valiant which was performed during the course of the whole war. Four colors were taken, one of which was that of the Spanish regiment, this being the first of that nationality which had ever been captured by Gustavus.

After going over the castle, whose capture would have tasked his resources and the valor of his troops to the utmost had he been compelled to attack it in the usual way, Gustavus sent for the officers of Ramsay's companies and thanked them individually for their capture.

"What! you here, Malcolm Græme!" Gustavus said as he came in at the rear of Ramsay's officers. "Why, what had you to do with this business?"

"I was only a volunteer, sire," Malcolm said. "I crossed with the parties who fetched the boats; but as my instructions ended there I had nought to do, and finding that Ramsay's men were about to march up to the attack of the castle, I thought it best to join them, being somewhat afraid to stop in the town alone."

"And he did valiant service, sire," the major said. "I marked him in the thick of the fight, and saw more than one Imperialist go down before his sword."

"You know the story of the pitcher and the well, Captain Græme," the king said, smiling. "Some day you will go once too often, and I shall have to mourn the loss of one of the bravest young officers in my army."

There was no rest for the soldiers of Gustavus, and no sooner had Oppenheim fallen than the army marched against Maintz. This was defended by two thousand Spanish troops under Don Philip de Sylvia, and was a place of immense strength. It was at once invested, and trenches commenced on all sides, the Green Brigade as usual having the post of danger and honor facing the citadel. The investment began in the evening, but so vigorously did the Scotch work all night in spite of the heavy musketry and artillery fire with which the garrison swept the ground that by morning the first parallel was completed, and the soldiers were under shelter behind a thick bank of earth.

All day the Imperialists kept up their fire, the Scots gradually pushing forward their trenches. In the evening Colonel Axel-Lilly, one of the bravest of the Swedish officers, came into the trenches to pay a visit to Hepburn. He found him just sitting down to dinner with Munro by the side of a fire in the trench. They invited him to join them, and the party were chatting gayly when a heavy cannon ball crashed through the earthen rampart behind them and, passing between Hepburn and Munro, carried off the leg of the Swedish officer.

Upon the following day the governor, seeing that the Swedes had erected several strong batteries, and that the Green Brigade, whose name was a terror to the Imperialists, was preparing to storm, capitulated, and his soldiers were allowed to march out with all their baggage, flying colors, and two pieces of cannon. Eighty pieces of cannon fell into the hands of the Swedes. The citizens paid 220,000 dollars as the ransom of their city from pillage, and the Jews 180,000 for the protection of their quarters and of their gorgeous synagogue, whose wealth and magnificence were celebrated; and on the 14th of December, 1631, on which day Gustavus completed his thirty-seventh year, he entered the city as conqueror.

Here he kept Christmas with great festivity, and his court was attended by princes and nobles from all parts of Germany. Among them were six of the chief princes of the empire and twelve ambassadors from foreign powers. Among the nobles was the count of Mansfeld, who brought with him his wife and daughter. Three days before Christmas Hepburn's brigade had been moved in from their bivouac in the snow-covered trenches, and assigned quarters in the town, and the count, who arrived on the following day, at once repaired to the mansion inhabited by the colonel and officers of Munro's regiment, and inquired for Malcolm Græme.

"You will find Captain Græme within," the Scottish soldier on sentry said.

"It is not Captain Græme I wish to see," the count said, "but Malcolm Græme, a very young officer."

"I reckon that it is the captain," the soldier said; "he is but a boy; but in all the regiment there is not a braver soldier, not even the colonel himself. Donald," he said, turning to a comrade, "tell Captain Græme that he is wanted here."

In a short time Malcolm appeared at the door.

"Ah! it is you, my young friend!" the count exclaimed; "and you have won the rank of captain already by your brave deeds! Right glad am I to see you again. I have come with my wife to attend the court of this noble king of yours. Can you come with me at once? The countess is longing to see you, and will be delighted to hear that you have passed unscathed through all the terrible contests in which you have been engaged. My daughter is here too; she is never tired of talking about her young Scottish soldier; but now that you are a captain she will have to be grave and respectful."

Malcolm at once accompanied the count to his house, and was most kindly received by the countess.

"It is difficult to believe," she said, "that 'tis but four months since we met, so many have been the events which have been crowded into that time. Scarce a day has passed but we have received news of some success gained, of some town or castle captured, and your Green Brigade has always been in the van. We have been constantly in fear for you, and after that terrible battle before Leipzig Thekla scarcely slept a wink until we obtained a copy of the *Gazette* with the names of the officers killed."

"You are kind indeed to bear me so in remembrance," Malcolm said, "and I am indeed grateful for it. I have often wondered whether any fresh danger threatened you; but I hoped that the advance of the marquis of Hamilton's force would have given the Imperialists too much to do for them to disturb you."

"Yes, we have had no more trouble," the countess replied. "The villages which the Imperialists destroyed are rising again; and as after the flight of the enemy the cattle and booty they had captured were all left behind, the people are recovering from their visit. What terrible havoc has the war caused! Our way here led through ruined towns and villages, the country is infested by marauders, and all law and order is at an end save where there are strong bodies of troops. We rode with an escort of twenty men; but even then we did not feel very safe until we were fairly through Franconia. And so you have passed unwounded through the strife?"

"Yes, countess," Malcolm replied. "I had indeed a ball through my leg at Würtzburg; but as it missed the bone, a trifle like that is scarcely worth counting. I have been most fortunate indeed."

"Here is a captain now," the count said, "and to obtain such promotion he must have greatly distinguished himself. I do not suppose that he will himself tell us his exploits; but I shall soon learn all about them from others. I am to meet his colonel this evening at a dinner at the palace and shall be able to give you the whole history to-morrow."

"But I want the history now," Thekla said. "It is much nicer to hear a thing straight from some one who has done it than from any one else."

"There is no story to tell," Malcolm said. "I had been promised my lieutenancy at the first vacancy before I was at Mansfeld, and on my return found that the vacancy had already occurred, and I was appointed. I got my company the other day for a very simple matter, namely for swimming across the Rhine with a barrel fixed on each side of me to prevent my sinking. Nothing very heroic about that, you see, young lady."

"For swimming across the Rhine!" the count said. "Then you must have been the Scottish officer who with a sergeant swam and fetched the boat across which enabled the Swedes to pass a body of troops over, and so open the way into the Palatinate. I heard it spoken of as a most gallant action."

"I can assure you," Malcolm said earnestly, "that there was no gallantry about it. It was exceedingly cold, I grant, but that was all."

"Then why should the king have made you a captain for it? You can't get over that."

"That was a reward for my luck," Malcolm laughed. "'Tis better to be lucky than to be rich, it is said, and I had the good luck to discover a boat concealed among the bushes just at the time when a boat was worth its weight in gold."

For an hour Malcolm sat chatting and then took his leave as he was going on duty, promising to return the next day, and to spend as much of his time as possible with them while they remained in the city.

CHAPTER XII.

THE PASSAGE OF THE LECH.

For the next two months the Green Brigade remained quietly at Maintz, a welcome rest after their arduous labors. The town was very gay, and every house was occupied either by troops or by the nobles and visitors from all parts of northern Europe. Banquets and balls were of nightly occurrence; and a stranger who arrived in the gay city would not have dreamed that a terrible campaign had just been concluded, and that another to the full as arduous was about to commence.

During this interval of rest the damages which the campaign had effected in the armor and accoutrements of men and officers were repaired, the deep dents effected by sword, pike and bullet were hammered out, the rust removed, and the stains of blood and bivouac obliterated; fresh doublets and jerkins were served out from the ample stores captured from the enemy, and the army looked as gay and brilliant as when it first landed in North Germany.

Malcolm spent much of his spare time with the count and countess of Mansfeld, who, irrespective of their gratitude for the assistance he had rendered them in time of need, had taken a strong liking to the young Scotchman.

"You are becoming quite a court gallant, Graeme," one of his comrades said at a court festival where Malcolm had been enjoying himself greatly, having, thanks to the countess of Mansfeld, no lack of ladies, while many of the officers were forced to look on without taking part, the number of ladies being altogether insufficient to the throng of officers, Swedish, German and Scottish. Beyond the scarf and feathers which showed the brigade to which officers belonged, there was, even when in arms, but slight attempt at uniformity in their attire, still less so when off duty. The scene at these celebrations was therefore gay in the extreme, the gallants all being attired in silk, satin or velvet of brilliant colors slashed with white or some contrasting hue. The tailors at Maintz had had a busy time of it, for in so rapid a campaign much baggage had necessarily been lost, and many of the officers required an entirely new outfit before they could take part in the court festivities.

There was, however, no lack of money, for the booty and treasure captured had been immense, and each officer having received a fixed share, they were well able to renew their wardrobes. Some fresh reinforcements arrived during their stay here, and the vacancies which battle and disease had made in the ranks were filled up.

But although the Green Brigade did not march from Maintz until the 5th of March, 1632, the whole army did not enjoy so long a rest. In February Gustavus despatched three hundred of Ramsay's regiment under Lieutenant-Colonel George Douglas against the town of Creutznach, together with a small party of English volunteers under Lord Craven. Forty-seven of the men were killed while opening the trenches, but the next day they stormed one of the gates and drove the garrison, which was composed of six hundred Walloons and Burgundians, out of the town into the castle of Kausemberg, which commanded it. Its position was extremely strong, its walls and bastions rising one behind another, and their aspect was so formidable that they were popularly known as the "Devil's Works." From these the garrison opened a very heavy fire into the town, killing many of the Scots. Douglas, however, gave them but short respite, for gathering his men he attacked the castle and carried bastion after bastion by storm until the whole were taken.

About the same time the important town of Ulm on the Danube opened its gates to the Swedes, and Sir Patrick Ruthven was appointed commandant, with twelve hundred Swedes as garrison. Colonel Munro with two companies of musketeers marched to Coblentz and aided Otto Louis, the Rhinegrave, who with a brigade of twenty troops of horse was expecting to be attacked by ten thousand Spaniards and Walloons from Spires. Four regiments of Spanish horse attacked the Rhinegrave's quarters, but were charged so furiously by four troops of

Swedish dragoons under Captain Hume that three hundred of them were killed and the elector of Nassau taken prisoner; after this the Spaniards retired beyond the Moselle.

In other parts of Germany the generals of Gustavus were equally successful. General Horn defeated the Imperialists at Heidelberg and Heilbronn. General Löwenhausen scoured all the shores of the Baltic, and compelled Colonel Graham, a Scotch soldier in the Imperial service, to surrender the Hanse town of Wismar. Graham marched out with his garrison, three thousand strong, with the honors of war *en route* for Silesia, but having, contrary to terms, spiked the cannon, plundered the shipping, and slain a Swedish lieutenant, Löwenhausen pursued him, and in the battle which ensued five hundred of Graham's men were slain and the colonel himself with two thousand taken prisoner.

General Ottentodt was moving up the Elbe carrying all before him with a force of fourteen thousand men, among whom were five battalions of Scots and one of English. This force cleared the whole duchy of Mecklenburg, capturing all the towns and fortresses in rapid succession. Sir Patrick Ruthven advanced along the shores of Lake Constance, driving the Imperialists before him into the Tyrol. Magdeburg was captured by General Banner, the landgrave of Hesse-Cassel reduced all Fulda-Paderborn and the adjacent districts, the elector of Saxony overran Bohemia, and Sir Alexander Leslie threatened the Imperialists in Lower Saxony.

Thus the campaign of 1632 opened under the most favorable auspices. The Green Brigade marched on the 5th of March to Aschaffenburg, a distance of more than thirty miles, a fact which speaks volumes for the physique and endurance of the troops, for this would in the present day be considered an extremely long march for troops, and the weight of the helmet and armor, musket and accoutrements of the troops of those days was fully double that now carried by European soldiers. Here they were reviewed by the king.

By the 10th the whole army, twenty-three thousand strong, were collected at Weinsheim and advanced toward Bavaria, driving before them the Imperialists under the Count de Bucquio. The Chancellor Oxenstiern had been left by the king with a strong force to guard his conquests on the Rhine.

No sooner had the king marched than the Spaniards again crossed the Moselle. The chancellor and the duke of Weimar advanced against them. The Dutch troops, who formed the first line of the chancellor's army, were unable to stand the charge of the Spanish and fled in utter confusion; but the Scottish regiment of Sir Roderick Leslie, who had succeeded Sir John Hamilton on his resignation, and the battalion of Sir John Ruthven charged the Spaniards with leveled pikes so furiously that these in turn were broken and driven off the field.

On the 26th of March Gustavus arrived before the important town and fortress of Donauwörth, being joined on the same day by the laird of Foulis with his two regiments of horse and foot. Donauwörth is the key to Suabia; it stands on the Danube, and was a strongly fortified place, its defenses being further covered by fortifications upon a lofty eminence close by, named the Schellemberg. It was held by the duke of Saxe-Lauenburg with two thousand five hundred men.

The country round Donauwörth is fertile and hilly, and Gustavus at once seized a height which commanded the place. The Bavarians were at work upon entrenchments here as the Swedes advanced, but were forced to fall back into the town. From the foot of the hill a suburb extended to the gates of the city. This was at once occupied by five hundred musketeers, who took up their post in the houses along the main road in readiness to repel a sortie should the garrison attempt one; while the force on the hillside worked all night, and by daybreak on the 27th had completed and armed a twenty-gun battery.

In this was placed a strong body of infantry under Captain Semple, a Scotchman. As this battery commanded the walls of the town and flanked the bridge across the Danube, the position of the defenders was now seriously menaced, but the duke of Saxe-Lauenburg refused the demand of Gustavus to surrender. The battery now opened fire, first demolishing a large stone building by the river occupied by a force of Imperialists, and then directing its fire upon the city gates.

The cannonade continued after nightfall, but in the darkness a body of Imperialist horsemen under Colonel Cronenberg dashed out at full speed through the gate, cut a passage through the musketeers in the suburb, galloped up the hill, and fell upon the infantry and artillery in the battery. So furious was their charge that the greater part of the defenders of the battery were cut down. The guns were spiked, and the cavalry, having accomplished their purpose, charged down the hill, cut their way through the suburb, and regained the town.

This gallant exploit deranged the plans of the Swedes. Gustavus reconnoitered the town accompanied by Sir John Hepburn, and by the advice of that officer decided upon a fresh plan of operations. Hepburn pointed out to him that by taking possession of the angle formed by the confluence of the Wermitz and Danube to the west of the town, the bridge crossing from Donauwörth into Bavaria would be completely commanded, and the garrison would be cut off from all hope of escape and of receiving relief from Bavaria.

The plan being approved, Hepburn drew off his brigade with its artillery, and marching five miles up the Danube crossed the river at the bridge of Hassfurt and descended the opposite bank until he faced Donauwörth. He reached his position at midnight and placed his cannon so as to command the whole length of the bridge, and then posted his musketeers in the gardens and houses of a suburb on the river so that their cross fire also swept it.

The pikemen were drawn up close to the artillery at the head of the bridge. Quietly as these movements were performed the garrison took the alarm, and toward morning the duke, finding his retreat intercepted, sallied out at the head of eight hundred musketeers to cut his way through; but as the column advanced upon the bridge the Green Brigade opened fire, the leaden hail of their musketeers smote the column on both sides, while the cannon plowed lanes through it from end to end. So great was the destruction that the Bavarians retreated in confusion back into the town again, leaving the bridge strewn with their dead.

Alone the gallant duke of Saxe-Lauenburg charged through the hail of fire across the bridge, fell upon the pikemen sword in hand and, cutting his way through them, rode away, leaving his garrison to their fate. The roar of artillery informed Gustavus what was going on, and he immediately opened fire against the other side of the town and led his men to the assault of the gate.

The instant the Scotch had recovered from their surprise at the desperate feat performed by the duke, Hepburn, calling them together, placed himself at their head and led them across the bridge. The panic-stricken fugitives had omitted to close the gate and the Scotch at once entered the town. Here the garrison resisted desperately; their pikemen barred the streets, and from every window and roof their musketeers poured their fire upon the advancing column.

The day was breaking now and the roar of battle in the city mingled with that at the gates, where the Swedes were in vain striving to effect an entrance. Gradually the Scotch won their way forward; five hundred of the Bavarians were killed, in addition to four hundred who had fallen on the bridge. The rest now attempted to fly. Great numbers were drowned in the Danube and the remainder were taken prisoners. The streets were encumbered by the heavily-laden baggage-wagons, and a vast amount of booty fell into the hands of the Scotch, who thus became masters of the town before Gustavus and his Swedes had succeeded in carrying the gate.

The king now entered the town, and as soon as order was restored Hepburn's brigade recrossed the Danube and threw up a strong work on the other side of the bridge; for Tilly was on the Lech, but seven miles distant, and might at any moment return. He had just struck a severe blow at Marshal Horn, who had recently taken Bamberg. His force, nine thousand strong, had been scattered to put down a rising of the country people, when Tilly with sixteen thousand fell upon them.

A column under Bauditzen was attacked and defeated, and Tilly's horsemen pursued them hotly to the bridge leading to the town. Marshal Horn threw a barricade across this and defended it until nightfall. Tilly had then fallen back before the advance of Gustavus to a very strong position on the Lech. This was an extremely rapid river, difficult to cross and easily defensible. Tilly had broken down the bridges, and was prepared to dispute till the last the further advance of the Swedes. He placed his army between Rain, where the Lech falls into the Danube, and Augsburg, a distance of sixteen miles—all the assailable points being strongly occupied, with small bodies of cavalry in the intervals to give warning of the approach of the enemy. He had been joined by Maximilian of Bavaria, and his force amounted to forty thousand men.

Gustavus gave his army four days' rest at Donauwörth, and then advanced with thirty-two thousand men against the Lech. His dragoons, who had been pushed forward, had found the bridges destroyed. He first attempted to repair that at Rain, but the fire of the artilley and musketry was so heavy that he was forced to abandon the idea. He then made a careful reconnoissance of the river, whose course was winding and erratic.

Finding that at every point at which a crossing could be easily effected Tilly's batteries and troops commanded the position, he determined to make his attack at a point where the river made a sharp bend in the form of a semi-circle, of which he occupied the outer edge. He encamped the bulk of his army at the village of Nordheim, a short distance in the rear, and erected three powerful batteries mounting seventy-two guns. One of these faced the center of the loop, the others were placed opposite the sides.

The ground on the Swedish bank of the river was higher than that facing it; and when the Swedish batteries opened they so completely swept the ground inclosed by the curve of the river that the Imperialists could not advance across it and were compelled to remain behind a rivulet called the Ach, a short distance in the rear of the Lech. They brought up their artillery, however, and replied to the cannonade of the Swedes.

For four days the artillery duel continued, and while it was going on a considerable number of troops were at work in the village of Oberndorf, which lay in a declivity near the river, hidden from the sight of the Imperialists, constructing a bridge. For that purpose a number of strong wooden trestles of various heights and with feet of unequal length for standing in the bed of the river, were prepared together with a quantity of piles to be driven in among and beside them to enable them to resist the force of the current.

On the night of the fourth day the king caused a number of fires to be lighted near the river, fed with green wood and damp straw. A favorable wind blew the smoke toward the enemy and thus concealed the ground from them. At daybreak on the 5th of April a thousand picked men crossed the river in two boats and, having reached the other side, at once proceeded to throw up intrenchments to cover the head of the bridge, while at the same time the workmen began to place the trestles in position.

As soon as day broke Tilly became aware of what was being done, and two batteries opened fire upon the work at the head of the bridge and against the bridge itself; but the low and swampy nature of the ground on the Imperialist side of the river prevented his placing the batteries in a position from which they could command the works, and their fire proved ineffective in preventing the construction of the bridge. Seeing this, Tilly at once commenced preparations for arresting the further advance of the Swedes.

To reach his position they would be obliged to cross the swampy ground exposed to the fire of his troops, and to render their progress still more difficul t he proceeded to cut down large trees, lopping and sharpening their branches to form a *chevaux-de-frise* before his troops. All the morning a heavy cannonade was kept up on both sides, but by noon the bridge was completed and the advance-guard of the Swedes, led by Colonels Wrandel and Gassion, advanced across it. As the other brigades were following, Tilly directed General Altringer to lead his cavalry against them.

Altringer led his troops round the end of the marsh and charged with great bravery down upon the Swedes. These, however, had time to form up, and a tremendous fire of musketry was poured into the Imperialist horse, while the round shot from the three Swedish batteries plowed their ranks in front and on both flanks. Under such circumstances, although fighting with reckless bravery, the Imperialist cavalry were repulsed. Altringer, however, rallied them and led them back again to the charge, but a cannon ball grazed his temple and he was carried senseless from the field. His men, shaken by the tremendous fire and deprived of their leader, fell back in confusion.

Tilly at once placed himself at the head of a chosen body of troops and advanced to the attack, fighting with the ardor and bravery which always distinguished him. He was short in stature and remarkable for his ugliness as well as his bravery. Lean and spare in figure, he had hollow cheeks, a long nose, a broad wrinkled forehead, heavy mustaches, and a sharp-pointed chin. He had from his boyhood been fighting against the Protestants. He had learned the art of war under the cruel and pitiless Spanish general, Alva, in the Netherlands, of which country he was a native, and had afterward fought against them in Bavaria, in Bohemia, and the Palatinate, and had served in Hungary against the Turks.

Until he met Gustavus at Breitenfeld he had never known a reverse. A bigoted Catholic, he had never hesitated at any act of cruelty which might benefit the cause for which he fought, or strike terror into the Protestants; and the singularity of his costume and the ugliness of his appearance heightened the terror which his deeds inspired among them. When not in armor his costume was modeled upon that of the duke of Alva, consisting of a slashed doublet of green silk, with an enormously wide-brimmed and high conical hat adorned with a large red ostrich feather. In his girdle he carried a long dagger and a Toledo sword of immense length. His personal bravery was famous, and never did he fight more gallantly than when he led his veterans to the attack of the Swedes.

For twenty minutes a furious hand-to-hand conflict raged, and the result was still uncertain when a shot from a falconet struck Tilly on the knee and shattered the bone, and the old general fell insensible to the ground. He was carried off the field, and his troops, now without a leader, gave way, the movement being hastened by two bodies of Swedish horse, who, eager for action, swam their horses across the river and threatened to cut off the retreat. By this time evening was at hand. The Swedes had secured the passage of the river, but the Imperialist army still held its intrenched position in the wood behind the Lech. Gustavus brought the rest of his army across and halted for the night.

The Imperialist position was tremendously strong, being unassailable on the right and covered in the front by the marshy ground. It could still have been defended with every prospect of success by a determined general, but the two best Imperialist commanders were *hors de combat*, and Maximilian of Bavaria, the nominal generalissimo, had no military experience. The army, too, was disheartened by the first success of the Swedes and by the loss of the general whom they regarded as well-nigh invincible.

Tilly had now recovered his senses, but was suffering intense agony from his wound, and on being consulted by Maximilian he advised him to fall back, as the destruction of his army would leave the whole country open to the Swedes.

The Imperialists accordingly evacuated their position and fell back in good order during the night on Neuberg, and then to Ingolstadt. Rain and Neuberg were occupied the next day by the Swedes. Gustavus despatched Marshal Horn to follow the retreating enemy to Ingolstadt, and he himself with the rest of his army marched up the Lech to Augsburg, which was held by Colonel Breda with four thousand five hundred men.

The Imperialists had broken down the bridge, but Gustavus immediately built two others, one above and the other below the city, and summoned it to surrender. Breda, hearing that Tilly was dying, Altringer severely wounded, and that no help was to be expected from Maximilian, considered it hopeless to resist, and surrendered the town, which Gustavus, attended by the titular king of Bohemia and many other princes, entered in triumph on the following day, April 14th.

The capture of Augsburg was hailed with peculiar satisfaction, as the city was regarded as the birthplace of the Reformation in Germany. Leaving a garrison there the king retraced his steps along the Lech to Neuberg, and marched thence to join Marshal Horn in front of Ingolstadt.

This town was one of the strongest places in Ger

many and had never been captured. It was now held by a formidable garrison, and the Imperialist army covered it on the north. Tilly had implored Maximilian to defend it and Ratisbon at all hazards, as their possession was a bar to the further advance of Gustavus.

The king arrived before it on the 19th, and on the following day advanced to reconnoiter it closely. The gunners of the town, seeing a number of officers approaching, fired, and with so good an aim that a cannon ball carried off the hind-quarters of the horse the king was riding. A cry of alarm and consternation burst from the officers, but their delight was great when the king rose to his feet, covered with dust and blood indeed, but otherwise unhurt.

On the following day a cannon ball carried off the head of the margave of Baden-Durlach, and on the same day Tilly expired. With his last breath he urged Maximilian never to break his alliance with the emperor, and to appoint Colonel Cratz, an officer of great courage and ability, to the command of his army.

Gustavus remained eight days before Ingolstadt and then, finding that the reduction of the place could not be effected without the loss of much valuable time, he raised the siege. On his march he took possession of Landshut and forced it to pay a ransom of one hundred thousand thalers and to receive a garrison, and then continued his way to Munich.

The Bavarian capital surrendered without a blow on the 17th of May. Gustavus made a triumphal entry into the town, where he obtained possession of a vast quantity of treasure and stores. Here he remained some little time reducing the country round and capturing many cities and fortresses. The Green Brigade had suffered severally at Ingolstadt. On the evening of the 19th of April the king, expecting a sally, had ordered Hepburn to post the brigade on some high ground near the gate, and the soldiers remained under arms the whole night.

The glow of their matches enabled the enemy to fire with precision, and a heavy cannonade was poured upon them throughout the whole night. Three hundred men were killed as they stood, Munro losing twelve men by one shot; but the brigade stood their ground unflinchingly, and remained until morning in steady line, in readiness to repel any sortie of the enemy.

The army suffered greatly on the march from the Lech to Ingolstadt, and thence to Munich, from the attacks of the country people, who were excited against them by the priests. Every straggler who fell into their hands was murdered with horrible cruelty, the hands and feet being cut off, and other savage mutilations being performed upon them; in revenge for which the Swedes and Scots shot all the Bavarians who fell into their hands, and burned two hundred towns and villages.

CHAPTER XIII.

CAPTURED BY THE PEASANTS.

MALCOLM GRÆME was not present at the siege of Ingolstadt. The orders after crossing the Lech had been very strict against straggling, so soon as the disposition of the country people was seen; but it is not easy to keep a large column of troops in a solid body. The regiments on the march indeed, under the eye of the officers, can be kept in column, but a considerable number of troops are scattered along the great convoy of wagons containing the tents, stores, and ammunition of the army, and which often extends some miles in length. Even if the desire for plunder does not draw men away, many are forced to fall behind either from sickness, sore feet, or other causes.

The number of these was comparatively small in the army of Gustavus, for discipline was strict and the spirit of the troops good. As soon, however, as it was found that every straggler who fell into the hands of the peasantry was murdered under circumstances of horrible atrocity it became very difficult for the officers to keep the men together, so intense was their fury and desire for vengeance against the savage peasantry, and on every possible occasion when a village was seen near the line of march men would slip away and slay, plunder, and burn.

Gustavus endeavored to repress these proceedings. He shared the indignation of his troops at the barbarous conduct of the peasantry, but throughout the war he always tried to carry on hostilities so as to inflict as little loss and suffering as possible upon non-combatants. This state of warfare too between his troops and the country people added to his difficulties, for the peasantry drove off their cattle and burned their stacks, and rendered it necessary for provisions and forage to be carried with the army. Parties were therefore sent out on the flanks of the column for the double purpose of preventing soldiers stealing off to plunder and burn, and of picking up stragglers and saving them from the fury of the peasants.

A strong rear-guard followed a short distance behind the army. It was accompanied by some empty wagons, in which those who fell out and were unable to keep up with the march were placed. Two days after the advance from the Lech, Malcolm was in charge of a small party on the right flank of the column. There was no fear of an attack from the enemy, for the Swedish horsemen were out scouring the country, and the Imperialists were known to have fallen back to Ingolstadt. The villages were found deserted by the male inhabitants, the younger women too had all left, but a few old crones generally remained in charge. These scowled at the invaders, and crossing themselves muttered curses beneath their breath upon those whom their priests had taught them to regard as devils. There was nothing to tempt the cupidity of the soldiers in these villages. Malcolm's duty was confined to a casual inspection, to see that no stragglers had entered for the purpose of procuring wine.

The day's march was nearly over when he saw some flames rise from a village a short distance away. Hurrying forward with his men he found a party of ten of the Swedish soldiers who had stolen away from the baggage guard engaged in plundering. Two peasants lay dead in the street, and a house was in flames.

Malcolm at once ordered his detachment, who were twenty strong, to arrest the Swedes and to march them back to the columns. While they were doing this he went from house to house to see that none of the party were lurking there. At the door of the last house of the village three women were standing.

"Are any of the soldiers here?" he asked.

The women gave him an unintelligible answer in the country patois, and passing between them he entered the cottage. On the table stood a large jug of water, and lifting it he took a long draught. There was a sudden crash, and he fell heavily, struck down from behind with a heavy mallet by one of the women. He was stunned by the blow, and when he recovered his senses he found that he was bound hand and foot, a cloth had been stuffed tightly into his mouth, and he was covered thickly with a heap of straw and rubbish. He struggled desperately to free himself, but so tightly were the cords bound that they did not give in the slightest.

A cold perspiration broke out on his forehead as he reflected that he was helpless in the power of these savage peasants, and that he should probably be put to death by torture. Presently he could hear the shouts of his men, who, on finding that he did not return, had scattered through the village in search of him. He heard the voice of his sergeant.

"These old hags say they saw an officer walk across to the left. The captain may have meant us to march the prisoners at once to the column, and be waiting just outside the village for us, but it is not likely. At any rate, lads, we will search every house from top to bottom before we leave. So set to work at once; search every room, cupboard and shed. There may be foul play; though we see no men about, some may be in hiding."

Malcolm heard the sound of footsteps, and the crashing of planks as the men searched the cottages, wrenched off the doors of cupboards, and ransacked the whole place. Gradually the sound ceased, and everything became quiet. Presently he heard the sound of drums, and knew that the regiment which formed the rear-guard was passing.

It was bitterness indeed to know that his friends were within sound of a call for aid, and that he was bound and helpless. The halting-place for the night was, he knew, but a mile or two in advance, and his only hope was that some band of plunderers might in the night visit the village; but even then his chances of being discovered were small indeed, for even should they sack and burn it he would pass unnoticed lying hidden in the straw-yard. His captors were no doubt aware of the possibility of such a visit, for it was not until broad daylight, when the army would again be on its forward march, that they uncovered him.

Brave as Malcolm was he could scarce repress a shudder as he looked at the band of women who surrounded him. All were past middle age, some were old and toothless, but all were animated by a spirit of ferocious triumph. Raising him into a sitting position, they clustered round him, some shook their skinny hands in his face, others heaped curses upon him, some of the most furious assailed him with heavy sticks, and had he not still been clothed in his armor, would then and there have killed him.

This, however, was not their intention, for they intended to put him to death by slow torture. He was lifted and carried into the cottage. There the lacings of his armor were cut, the cords loosened one by one, sufficient to enable them to remove the various pieces of which it was composed, then he was left to himself, as the hags intended to postpone the final tragedy until the men returned from the hills.

This might be some hours yet, as the Swedish cavalry would still be scouring the country, and other bodies of troops might be marching up. From the conversation of the women, which he understood but imperfectly, Malcolm gathered that they thought the men would return that night. Some of the women were in favor of executing the vengeance themselves, but the majority were of opinion that the men should have their share of the pleasure.

All sorts of fiendish propositions were made as to the manner in which his execution should be carried out, but even the mildest caused Malcolm to shudder in anticipation. His arms were bound tightly to his side at the elbows, and the wrists were fastened in front of him, his legs were tied at the knees and ankles. Sometimes he was left alone as the women went about their various avocations in the village, but he was so securely bound that to him as to them his escape appeared altogether impossible. The day passed heavily and slowly. The cloth had been removed from his mouth, but he was parched with thirst, while the tightly-bound cords cut deeply into his flesh.

He had once asked for water, but his request had been answered with such jeers and mockery that he resolved to suffer silently until the last. At length the darkness of the winter evening began to fall when a thought suddenly struck him. On the hearth a fire was burning; he waited until the women had again left the hut. He could hear their voices without as they talked with those in the next cottage. They might at any moment return, and it was improbable that they would again go out, for the cold was bitter, and they would most likely wait indoors for the return of the men.

This then was his last opportunity. He rolled himself to the fire, and with his teeth seized the end of one of the burning sticks. He raised himself into a sitting position, and with the greatest difficulty laid the burning end of the stick across the cords which bound his wrists. It seemed to him that they would never catch fire. The flesh scorched and frizzled, and the smoke rose up with that of the burning rope. The agony was intense, but it was for life, and Malcolm unflinchingly held the burning brand in its place until the cords flew asunder and his hands were free. Although almost mad with the pain, Malcolm sat to work instantly to undo the other ropes. As soon as one of his arms was free he seized a hatchet, which lay near him, and rapidly cut the rest. He was not a moment too soon, for as he cut the last knot he heard the sound of steps, and two women appeared at the door.

On seeing their prisoner standing erect with an axe in his hand they turned and fled shrieking loudly. It was well for Malcolm that they did so, for so stiff and numbed were his limbs that he could scarcely hold the axe, and the slightest push would have thrown him to the ground.

Some minutes passed before, by stamping his feet and rubbing his legs he restored circulation sufficiently to totter across the room. Then he seized a brand and thrust it into the thatch of the house, having first put on his helmet and placed his sword and pistols in his belt. His hands were too crippled and powerless to enable him to fasten on the rest of his armor. He knew that he had no time to lose. Fortunately the women would not know how weak and helpless he was, for had they returned in a body they could easily have overpowered him; but at any moment the men might arrive, and if he was found there by them his fate was sealed.

Accordingly as soon as he had fired the hut he made his way from the village as quickly as he could crawl along. He saw behind him the flames rising higher and higher. The wind was blowing keenly, and the fire spread rapidly from house to house, and by the time he reached the road along which the army had traveled the whole village was in flames. He felt that he could not travel far, for the intense sufferings which he had endured for twenty-four hours without food or water had exhausted his strength.

His limbs were swollen and bruised from the tightness of the cords, the agony of his burned wrists was terrible, and after proceeding slowly for about a mile he drew off from the broad trampled track which the army had made in passing, and dragging himself to a clump of trees a short distance from the road, made his way through some thick undergrowth and flung himself down. The night was intensely cold, but this was a relief to him rather than otherwise, for it alleviated the burning pain of his limbs while he kept handfuls of snow applied to his wrists.

Two hours after he had taken refuge he heard a number of men come along the road at a run. Looking through the bushes he could see by their figures against the snow that they were peasants, and had no doubt that they were the men of the village who had returned and at once started in pursuit of him.

An hour later, feeling somewhat relieved, he left his hiding-place and moved a mile away from the road, as he feared that the peasants, failing to overtake him, might, as they returned, search every possible hiding-place near it. He had no fear of the track being noticed, for the surface of the snow was everywhere marked by parties going and returning to the main body. He kept on until he saw a small shed. The door was unfastened; opening it he found that the place was empty, though there were signs that it was usually used as a shelter for cattle.

A rough ladder led to a loft. This was nearly full of hay. Malcolm threw himself down on this, and covering himself up thickly, felt the blood again begin to circulate in his limbs. It brought, however, such a renewal of his pain, that it was not until morning that fatigue overpowered his sufferings and he fell asleep.

It was late in the afternoon when he woke at the sound of shouts and hollooing. Springing to his feet he looked out between the cracks in the boards and saw a party of forty or fifty peasants passing close by the shed. They were armed with hatchets, scythes, and pikes. On the heads of four of the pikes were stuck gory heads, and in the center of the party were three prisoners, two Swedes and a Scot. These were covered with blood, and were scarcely able to walk, but were being urged forward with blows and pike-thrusts amid the brutal laughter of their captors.

Malcolm retired to his bed full of rage and sorrow. It would have been madness to have followed his first impulse to sally out sword in hand and fall upon the ruffians, as such a step would only have ensured his own death without assisting the captives.

"Hitherto," he said to himself, "I have ever restrained my men, and have endeavored to protect the peasants from violence; hencefoward, so long as we remain in Bavaria, no word of mine shall be uttered to save one of these murderous peasants. However, I am not with my company yet. The army is two marches ahead, and must by this time be in front of Ingolstadt. I have been two days without food, and see but little chance of getting any until I rejoin them, and the whole country between us is swarming with an infuriated peasantry. The prospect is certainly not a bright one. I would give a year's pay to hear the sound of a Swedish trumpet."

When darkness had fairly set in Malcolm started on his way again. Although his limbs still smarted from the wales and sores left by the cords they had now recovered their lissomeness; but he was weak from want of food and no longer walked with the free, elastic stride which distinguished the Scottish infantry. His wrists gave him great pain, being both terribly burned, and every movement of the hand sent a thrill of agony up the arm. He persisted, however, in frequently opening and clenching his hands, regardless of the pain, for he feared that did he not do so they would stiffen and he would be unable to grasp a sword. Fortunately the wounds were principally on the upper side of the thumbs, where the flesh was burned away to the bone, but the sinews and muscles of the wrists had to a great extent escaped.

He had not journeyed very far when he saw a light ahead and presently perceived the houses of a village. A fire was lit in the center, and a number of figures were gathered round it.

"Something is going on," Malcolm said to himself; "as likely as not they have got some unfortunate prisoner. Whatever it be, I will steal in and try to get some food. I cannot go much further without it; and as their attention is occupied, I may find a cottage empty."

Making his way round to the back of the houses, he approached one of the cottages in the rear. He lifted the latch of the door and opened it a little. All was still. With his drawn sword he entered. The room was empty; a fire burned on the hearth, and on the table were some loaves which had evidently been just baked. Malcolm fell upon one of them and speedily devoured it, and, taking a long draught of water from a skin hanging against the wall, he felt another man.

He broke another loaf in two and thrust the pieces into his doublet, and then sallied out from the cottage again. Still keeping behind the houses he made his way until he got within view of the fire. Here he saw a sight which thrilled him with horror. Some eight or ten peasants and forty or fifty women were yelling and shouting. Fastened against a post in front of the fire were the remains of a prisoner. His ears, nose, hands and feet were cut off, and he was slowly bleeding to death.

Four other men, bound hand and foot, lay close to the fire. By its flames Malcolm saw the green scarves that told they were Scotchmen of his own brigade, and he determined at once to rescue them or die in the attempt. He crept forward until he reached the edge of the road; then he raised his pistol and with a steady aim fired at on of the natives, who fell dead across the fire.

Another shot laid another beside him before the peasants recovered from their first surprise. Then with a loud shout in German, "Kill—kill! and spare none!" Malcolm dashed forward. The peasants, believing that they were attacked by a strong body, fled precipitately in all directions. Malcolm, on reaching the prisoners, instantly severed their bonds.

Malcolm fired at one of the natives and then with a loud shout dashed forward.—Page 230.
—*The Lion of the North.*

"Quick, my lads!" he exclaimed; "we shall have them upon us again in a minute."

The men in vain tried to struggle to their feet—their limbs were too numbed to bear them.

"Crawl to the nearest cottage!" Malcolm exclaimed; "we can hold it until your limbs are recovered."

He caught up from the ground some pikes and scythes which the peasants had dropped in their flight, and aided the men to make their way to the nearest cottage. They were but just in time; for the peasants, finding they were not pursued, had looked round, and seeing but one opponent had gained courage and were beginning to approach again. Malcolm barred the door and then turned to his companions. There were loaves on the shelves, and these he cut up and handed to them.

"Quick, lads!" he said; "stamp your legs and swing your arms, and get the blood in motion. I will keep these fellows at bay a few minutes longer."

He reloaded his pistols and fired through the door, at which the peasants were now hewing with axes. A cry and a heavy fall told him that one of the shots had taken effect. Suddenly there was a smell of smoke.

"They have fired the roof," Malcolm said. "Now, lads, each of you put a loaf of bread under his jerkin. There is no saying when we may get more. Now get ready and sally out with me. There are but six or eight men in the village, and they are no match for us. They only dared to attack us because they saw that you couldn't walk."

The door was opened, and headed by Malcolm the four Scotchmen dashed out. They were assailed by a shower of missiles by the crowd as they appeared, but as soon as it was seen that the men were on foot again the peasants gave way. Malcolm shot one and cut down another, and the rest scattered in all directions.

"Now, lads, follow me while we may," and Malcolm again took to the fields. The peasants followed for some distance, but when the soldiers had quite recovered the use of their limbs Malcolm suddenly turned on his pursuers, overtaking and killing two of them. Then he and his men again continued their journey, the peasants no longer following. When at some distance from the village he said:

"We must turn and make for the Lech again. It is no farther than it is to Ingolstadt, and we shall find friends there. These peasants will go on ahead and raise all the villagers against us, and we should never get through. What regiment do you belong to, lads?" for in the darkness he had been unable to see their faces.

"Your own, Captain Græme. We were in charge of one of the wagons with sick. The wheel came off, and we were left behind the convoy while we were mending it. As we were at work our weapons laid on the ground, some twenty men sprang out from some bushes hard by and fell upon us. We killed five or six of them, but were beaten down and ten of our number were slain. They murdered all the sick in the wagons and marched us away, bound, to this village where you found us. Sandy M'Alister they had murdered just as you came up, and we should have had a like horrible fate had you been a few minutes later. Eh, sir! but it's an awful death to be cut in pieces by these devils incarnate!"

"Well, lads," Malcolm said, "we will determine that they shall not take us alive again. If we are overtaken or met by any of these gangs of peasants we will fight till we die. None of us, I hope, are afraid of death in fair strife, but the bravest might well shrink from such a death as that of your poor comrade. Now let us see what arms we have between us."

Malcolm had his sword and pistols, two of the men had pikes, the other two scythes fastened to long handles.

"These are clumsy weapons," Malcolm said. "You had best fit short handles to them, so as to make them into double-handled swords."

They were unable to travel far, for all were exhausted with the sufferings they had gone through, but they kept on until they came upon a village which had been fired when the troops marched through. The walls of a little church were alone standing. It had, like the rest of the village, been burned, but the shell still remained.

"So far as I can see," Malcolm said, "the tower

has escaped. Had it been burned we should see through the windows. We may find shelter in the belfry."

On reaching the church they found that the entrance to the belfry tower was outside the church, and to this, no doubt, it owed its escape from the fire which had destroyed the main edifice. The door was strong and defied their efforts to break it in.

"I must fire my pistol through the lock," Malcolm said. "I do not like doing so, for the sound may reach the ears of any peasants in the neighborhood; but we must risk it, for the cold is extreme, and to lie down in the snow would be well-nigh certain death."

He placed his pistol to the keyhole and fired. The lock at once yielded and the party entered the door.

"Before we mount," Malcolm said, "let each pick up one of these blocks of stone which have fallen from the wall. We will wedge the door from behind, and can then sleep secure against a surprise."

When the door was closed one of the men, who was a musketeer, struck some sparks from a flint and steel on to a slow match which he carried in his jerkin, and by its glow they were enabled to look around them. The stone steps began to ascend close to the door, and by laying the stones between the bottom step and the door they wedged the latter firmly in its place. They then ascended the stairs, and found themselves in a room some ten feet square, in which hung the bell which had called the village to prayers. It hung from some beams which were covered with a boarded floor, and a rough ladder led to a trapdoor, showing that there was another room above. The floor of the room in which they stood was of stone.

"Now, lads," Malcolm said, "two of you make your way up that ladder and rip up some of the planks of the flooring. See if there are any windows or loopholes in the chamber above, and if so stuff your jerkins into them; we will close up those here. In a few minutes we will have a roaring fire; but we must beware lest a gleam of light be visible without, for this belfry can be seen for miles round.

Some of the boards were soon split up into fragments; but before the light was applied to them Malcolm carefully examined each window and loophole to be sure that they were perfectly stopped. Then the slow match was placed in the center of a number of pieces of dry and rotten wood. One of the men kneeling down blew lustily, and in a few seconds a flame sprang up. The wood was now heaped on, and a bright fire was soon blazing high.

A trapdoor leading out on to the flat top of the tower was opened for the escape of the smoke, and the party then seated themselves round the fire, under whose genial warmth their spirits speedily rose. They now took from their wallets the bread which they had brought away with them.

"Now," Malcolm said, "we are better off at present than our comrades who are sleeping in the snow round the watch fires; but for all that I would that we were with them, for we have a long and dangerous march before us. And now, lads, you can sleep soundly. There will be no occasion to place a watch, for the door is securely fastened; but at the first dawn of light we must be on our feet; for although I do not mean to march until nightfall, we must remove the stoppings from the windows, for should the eye of any passing peasant fall upon them, he will guess at once that someone is sheltering here, and may proceed to find out whether it be friend or foe."

Having finished half their bread, for Malcolm had warned them to save the other half for the next day, the men lay down round the fire, and soon all were fast asleep.